FINTAN FEDORA
and the
DIAMOND MASK

BY CLIVE GODDARD

First published by
Goddard Creative
2016

ISBN-13: 978 0 9956287 2 4

This book is dedicated to the many wonderful children, teachers and librarians I have had the pleasure to meet over the last few years and also to everyone who has sent me funny and entertaining letters about Fintan's adventures. Special thanks to all the schools who have invited me to visit and to those brave souls who have acted out Fintan scenes with me while wearing a silly hat.

Clifton Primary Hull • The Dragon School Oxford
Alderman Cogan Hull • Epsom Primary
Freeland School Witney • Headington Library Oxford
High Wycombe C of E • Coombe Hill Kingston Upon Thames
Hull Central Library • Kalgoorlie Primary WA
Barley Hill Primary Thame • Collingwood Primary Hull
Kidmore End Primary Reading • Oldham Library Centre
Loseley Fields Binscombe • Pearson Primary Hull
Northbourne Primary Didcot • St John's Wallingford
Pinewood School Bourton • Speenhamland Thatcham
St Charles Primary Hull • St Ebbes Oxford
St Francis Primary Cowley • St Simon's Stockport
Thatcham Park School • Thorngrove Highclere
Leicester Grammar Juniors • Westbrook Primary Leeds

Ongoing thanks to my son, Dylan for his help and to my wife, Amy for her proof reading skills. Also for saying she likes this book even better than the last one.

PROLOGUE

Something strange had fallen out of the Fedora family tree. It was a fourteen year old boy called Fintan, youngest son of Mr and Mrs Fedora. The boy was nothing like his parents who owned the Fedora Fancy Cake Company, and nothing like his annoying older brother or sister either. Unlike them, Fintan's passion didn't lie in the world of fondant fancies, fudge slices, or pink icing. He was an explorer! An adventurer! He lived for the thrill of the wild. The excitement of trekking through the wilderness in search of some lost treasure; battling the elements and beating the odds. Unfortunately he wasn't very good at it.

Fintan had no sense of direction, very little common sense and an unfortunate habit of breaking everything he touched. Saying that Fintan was a bit accident prone was like saying that maths was a bit boring or that skunks were a bit smelly. Disasters followed him everywhere he went. They waited for him round corners and jumped out at him from behind trees.

Luckily he had Gribley to look after him. Gribley, the Fedora family's butler, who accompanied him on his travels, was sensible, careful and resourceful. He was sort of the complete opposite of Fintan but together they made a great team. The two of them had crossed stormy oceans, struggled through muddy jungles, and paddled down piranha-infested rivers. They had climbed mountains and crossed continents. They had fought off ruthless villains, discovered wonderful unseen places and brought back fabulous treasures. Together they had survived unbearable heat, hunger, thirst and the world's most terrifying public toilets. And there was still an enormous amount of the wild world left to explore!

ONE

To protect their sanity, their windows and their fragile ornaments, Fintan Fedora's parents had sent their accident prone son away to boarding school. No one blamed them. It was the sensible thing to do with a disastrous boy like Fintan. Knotweed Manor School was just the place for him. It was a strict, old fashioned school with old fashioned ideas about education and discipline and was just the sort of place to keep a difficult boy under control. Unfortunately Fintan had been thrown out of plenty of schools before so there was no guarantee he would stay there for long.

Which is why Mr and Mrs Fedora weren't all that surprised when the Headmistress asked them to come into the school to discuss 'a little problem'.

Knotweed Manor was an impressively solid, old Victorian building crammed with oak staircases, and trophy cabinets. The hallways were crowded with shiny-faced boys on their way to rugby practice, algebra and Latin classes; every one of them straight-backed, starch-collared and double-barrelled. The whole school smelled of polished wood, cabbage and, of course, schoolboys which was a really revolting combination.

Mr and Mrs Fedora were escorted to the school office. By the look on the Headmistress's face, Fintan must have been up to something pretty serious.

"So..." sighed Mr Fedora taking out his cheque book, "What's the boy done this time?"

The Headmistress leaned across her desk and peered very seriously over her glasses, "I'm afraid he's finally gone too far, Mr Fedora. If it were just one incident we might be able to forgive him but it never seems to stop! You're aware, of course, that he melted the plumbing in the chemistry department by pouring sulphuric acid and formaldehyde down the sink?"

Mr and Mrs Fedora nodded sadly. They were still paying for the damage.

"And that he somehow managed to spill the school kitchen's entire supply of custard powder into the swimming pool?"

They hadn't been aware of this but it sounded like the sort of thing he would do.

"Then last week..." continued the Head,

She hesitated and seemed to shudder at the recollection, "He absolutely ruined morning assembly. The theme was nature conservation and we had asked the children to go out and find something interesting to share. Most of the children brought a jar of wildflowers or some tadpoles... Fintan brought a python."

Mr and Mrs Fedora sat in their uncomfortable wooden chairs and struggled to think of anything sensible to say.

"Pardon?" said Mrs Fedora eventually.

"An eight metre long reticulated python," said the Head looking pale and exhausted.

"But where on earth did he get it from?" stammered Sir Filbert, "Pythons don't live in Berkshire do they?"

"He says he 'borrowed it' from the zoo," explained the Head, "Apparently he left a note for the zookeeper then brought it to school on the bus. There was also an unfortunate accident when the bus driver fainted."

"Oh dear," said Mrs Fedora. There wasn't much else she could say.

"Then during assembly the snake escaped and ran amok. The music mistress had a panic attack when it attempted to swallow a first year boy. Several members of staff had to chase it away with chairs. I'm afraid the beast has been evading capture ever since and is still at large somewhere in the school."

As she spoke the sound of smashing crockery and a distant scream echoed down the corridor.

"However, this morning was the last straw," continued the Head, trying to keep her voice calm but failing, "Fintan's project on the First World War led him to experiment with homemade land-mines. At break-time he blew up most of the rugby pitch and half of the maths building."

Mr and Mrs Fedora winced. This explained why there had been three fire engines and a bomb disposal squad parked outside the school.

"I'm sorry," concluded the Head, "but we can't take it anymore! He'll have to be expelled."

TWO

"I'm really sorry!" declared Fintan sitting on the sofa surrounded by his whole family, "I'll pay you back I promise! I'll get a paper round or a weekend job at the supermarket or something, honest I will!"

Mr Fedora didn't look convinced. The bill for repairs had come to over a hundred thousand pounds, not to mention all the money they had wasted on the boy's school fees. Fintan would have to do fifty paper rounds a day for the rest of his life to find that sort of money. And anyway, he had been sacked from his last paper round after riding his bike into the canal and soaking all the newspapers.

Mrs Fedora was on the brink of tears. How was the family going to cope with Fintan loitering around the house all the time, getting in the way and breaking things? It was a nightmare come true!

"And what about the conference?" she sobbed, "What are we going to do with the boy while we're away?"

Mr Fedora went a bit grey in the face.

"Oh dear, I hadn't thought of that," he said.

The family had booked a three week trip to South Africa for the World Cake Manufacturers' Conference. It was a really important event. The older children, Flavian and Felicity who had grown up and joined the family business, were going too but would probably spend most of their time sitting by the pool getting a tan while Gribley brought them cold drinks.

Mr Fedora began flicking through his address book, "Isn't there a relative he could stay with? Surely there's someone we could ask?"

His wife shook her head. They had run out of aunties and uncles who were prepared to look after the boy. Poor Auntie Fiona was still in therapy as a result of his last visit and her poodle was still bright blue from the pot of paint he had spilled on it.

Mr Fedora closed his address book and looked distressed, "We can't just leave him here on his own!" he muttered, "Can we?"

"Of course we can!" said Felicity "He'd be *fine* on his own."

"Yeah but he'd probably burn the house down!" laughed Flavian.

"Or himself!" added Felicity, snorting at her own incredible wit.

His older brother and sister never said anything nice about him. Ever.

Fintan had been sitting on the sofa listening to this conversation with growing interest. The family were going to South Africa? It was the first he'd heard about it! This was brilliant news! Africa was the land of steamy jungles, massive open savannahs and scorching deserts. *Young Adventurer* magazine, his favourite monthly publication, was always writing stuff about Africa. It was a whole continent full of mysterious undiscovered valleys and amazing creatures. He had read loads of fascinating things about it; lost tribes, giant warthogs and rare underground cave monkeys. There was the mysterious, diamond-studded mask of King Zunu, as well as the terrifying Nogo Hills Monster that swallowed people alive! Africa was an explorer's dream!

His family had fallen quiet and were now staring awkwardly at each other. They had run out of ideas.

"So…" began Fintan, daring to sound a bit optimistic, "Does that mean I can go with you?"

THREE

Two weeks later Fintan's dream had come true. He was actually standing on African soil! Well, not soil exactly. He was standing on African polished marble. The family were checking into Hotel Impala, a huge stylish building on the edge of Johannesburg. Everything was modern and luxurious and made of tinted glass and shiny steel. The lobby was full of people wearing suits and ties talking about the cake business and biscuit investment opportunities. Outside there was a massive swimming pool full of sparkling water surrounded by comfy, white sofas and carved wooden animals. Fintan hated it.

"Oh it's fabulous!" squealed Felicity who didn't hate it at all.

"So authentic!" agreed Flavian dumping his bag on the reception floor for someone else to carry.

Fintan gazed around at all the fancy lighting, vases of flowers and enormous paintings of elephants. This wasn't proper Africa! This was some sort of tourist place! He would much rather have been staying in a traditional hut with a rough grass roof and dried earth walls decorated with tribal designs. He wanted to be out on the immense African plains with the fascinating tribal peoples and all that amazing wildlife. The only wildlife at Hotel Impala was stuffed!

He stared at the sad looking heads of lion, buffalo, and rhino mounted on wooden plaques, and felt impatient to see the real thing.

"Are you all right, Master Fintan, sir?" enquired Gribley, who was struggling to carry five of Felicity's suitcases, "You look troubled."

Fintan pulled a face, "It's a bit posh here isn't it, Gribs," he whispered.

Gribley raised a surprised eyebrow. "It is a five star hotel with conference facilities, sir," he said, "I believe it is supposed to be 'posh'."

"Must've cost a fortune!" added Fintan quietly, hoping his dad wouldn't hear.

"It *did* cost a fortune!" said his dad who had heard anyway, "And fitting you in at the last minute didn't help. The sooner you find a job the better, young man!"

"Sorry," mumbled Fintan.

It felt like he'd been apologising for weeks now and he still hadn't paid back any of the money. He *had* been trying to get a job though. Really hard! He had written to the BBC asking if they'd like him to present a travel show or read the news or something. They had said no. He had written to the Prime Minister asking if he needed any help running the country. Not even a reply! Ideally, of course, he wouldn't be getting a job at all. He would be out in the Nogo Hills searching for the mask of King Zunu which had been lost for centuries. It was said to be studded with the biggest diamonds in the world and was worth an absolute fortune! And anyway, Africa was famous for its diamonds. Even if he couldn't find the mask all he had to do was nip out into the bush for a while and find a few lying around on the ground!

One of the hotel's porters in a smart white uniform approached Mrs Fedora, "May I carry your bags, Madam?" he asked.

This was usually Gribley's job but Mrs Fedora thought the African man would appreciate the tip money.

"Oh, yes please," she said, smiling.

The porter escorted the whole family upstairs. Fintan's parents had the largest room, of course, while Gribley had the small one next door and Felicity had the one next to that. Fintan, it appeared, would be sharing with his horrible older brother, Flavian. Neither of them were very happy about it. Mrs. Fedora handed the porter a small tip which gave Fintan an idea. Maybe bag-carrying was a job he could do to earn a bit of cash! It wasn't quite as exciting as being a newsreader or a prime minister but he had to start somewhere.

"Why do I have to share a room with idiot boy?" moaned Flavian, "He's not even supposed to be here!"

The family sympathised but there was nothing they could do.

"Well, I'm having the bed, then!" blurted Flavian, elbowing his brother out of the way.

He barged into the room and flopped onto the large, comfy bed by the window.

"Little brother can have that one," he said pointing to a metal camping bed which had been crammed in behind the door, "He'll be happier with that anyway. He can pretend he's on one of his stupid jungle adventures!"

FOUR

The next morning Fintan wished more than ever that he *was* on one of his stupid jungle adventures. His bed had been creaky and his brother had kept him awake most of the night snoring and muttering. He'd once had a better night's sleep in the Amazon rainforest despite a torrential downpour and anacondas slithering over his sleeping bag. At least that had been exciting!

He wandered down to breakfast, bleary-eyed but looking forward to the day that lay ahead. Unfortunately it turned out to be the most boring day of his life. His parents went off to the cake conference while his brother and sister went and sat by the pool. All day! A whole day spent lying on sun-loungers reading magazines and squirting sun-cream over themselves. They were the most unbelievably boring humans on the planet!

The hotel's other guests weren't very interesting either. They were mostly tubby, old executives who were there to discuss the international cake business. Strudel-makers from Germany, Swiss roll specialists from Switzerland, and a group of waffle salesclerks from Belgium. There was also a boring family from Croydon who constantly moaned about how hot it was and how you couldn't get a decent cup of tea in Africa.

Fintan felt totally frustrated! The massive, magnificent African bush was just a few miles away and he was missing it! Somewhere out there cheetahs were chasing gazelles up trees. Baboons were wandering around showing their bright red bums, and herds of wild elephants were grazing on the peanut trees. He should be out there in the wild discovering amazing things, not stuck in a boring hotel with his boring family.

"Gribley, old chap," trilled Felicity waving her empty glass, "Be a darling and top this up, will you?"

"Of course, Miss," said Gribley, "And would you care to see a list of activities the hotel is offering? Apparently there are safari trips and–"

"Ugh, no!" snorted Felicity, "Seriously? Can you see *me* on a safari trip? It would absolutely ruin my shoes!"

Flavian felt the same way, "Not for us, Gribley, old man. Going near all those sweaty animals and flies and dung and things! Not a chance!"

"I'll go!" chimed in Fintan excitedly.

"Oh, no you won't!" said Felicity, "Dad says you can't do any trips unless you pay for them yourself!"

"Yeah, get a job you lazy bum!" sneered Flavian, enjoying another chance to be horrible to his little brother.

"Perhaps you might enjoy this activity," continued Gribley, handing glossy leaflets to Flavian and Felicity. "It's a balloon safari. One merely floats through the air in a hot air balloon enjoying the view and observing the wildlife from a safe distance. There is no risk of one's shoes being ruined."

Both of them glanced at the leaflet and looked surprisingly interested.

"A safe distance, you say?" pondered Flavian.

"Ooh," said Felicity suddenly sounding quite excited, "Who's this chap in the photo?"

She pointed at an image of a very handsome African man in a crisply pressed uniform with a broad, gleaming smile and dark twinkling eyes.

"I believe that is the balloon pilot, Miss," explained Gribley.

"The pilot!" gasped Felicity, "OMG he's gorgeous! Count me in!"

"Me, too," added Flavian, "It says there's champagne and tasty little snacks and everything! That's a bit more like it."

"And me. I'll go!" said Fintan, for completely different reasons.

Gribley shook his head sadly, "I'm afraid your father won't allow it, Master Fintan, sir."

"I tell you what," suggested Flavian while poking his little brother in the chest, "Seeing as I'm so generous, if you get me a drink right now I'll give you five pence."

Fintan frowned. It was seriously humiliating but he did it anyway. He needed all the money he could get.

FIVE

Fintan spent the rest of the day wandering around the hotel lobby trying to make some cash by carrying people's bags. It didn't seem fair but the hotel's proper porters seemed to get all the customers. Probably because they had smart uniforms, lovely manners and lifted people's cases rather than dragging them across the floor.

By evening he had carried about twenty bags but had only earned a total of five rand. A 'rand' was apparently what the South Africans called their money. And five of them were nowhere near enough for a balloon safari.

Just as he was about to give up he noticed an elderly lady with sparkly earrings striding angrily over to the reception desk. She rang the bell looking very impatient and very rich.

"Ah, good evening, Lady Van der Kloot," said the hotel receptionist, bowing slightly, "How may I help you?"

"Well, for a start you can do as you are told!" snapped the old lady, plonking her handbag down on the desk.

She opened the bag and pulled out a small silver tiara, studded with dozens of very sparkly diamonds.

"Now listen here," she went on, "I specifically asked for a room with a safe for my valuables and yet you have put me in a room without one! I demand that you move me to a room with a safe at once!"

The receptionist apologised for the terrible mistake, fussed around on her computer screen for a while, then apologised a bit more. The hotel was completely full. There was nothing she could do.

"Well, it's just not good enough! My diamond tiara is worth an absolute fortune!" insisted the old lady, placing the tiara back in her handbag and patting it protectively.

Fintan couldn't see what all the fuss was about. The diamonds were tiny! They were nowhere near as big as the ones in King Zunu's mask which, according to legend, were the size of golf balls. Lady Van der Kloot's diamonds were no bigger than peanuts!

Several people who had been wandering through the lobby suddenly stopped and listened. A diamond tiara? Worth an absolute fortune? And no safe to lock it up in? This really wasn't the sort of thing you should announce in a room full of strangers; especially not in such a loud voice!

"I shall hold you personally responsible if any harm comes to it," she concluded, wagging a scrawny finger at the receptionist.

As she turned to go back to her room, Fintan saw his chance. This old lady was obviously very rich and, if he was lucky, she might be a really good tipper, too!

"May I carry your bags for you, Madam?" he asked, stepping in front of her and smiling a big, friendly smile.

The old lady stared down at him as if he were something nasty stuck to her shoe, "Who the devil are you, child?" she said acidly, "Do you work here?"

"Well, not officially," admitted Fintan, "I'm just sort of helping out."

She tutted and shook her head, making the loose skin on her face wobble, "You, young man, are an imbecile!" she sneered, "If you had any sense in your head you would see that I don't have any bags. They are already in my room!"

"What about this one then?" asked Fintan reaching for her small sparkly handbag, "I could carry that if you like?"

To his surprise Lady Van der Kloot let out a shriek and clutched the bag to her chest.

"Get away, you horrid boy!" she yelled, "Don't you dare touch my bag!"

Without taking her furious eyes off him for a second, Lady Van der Kloot edged away and took the lift back to her room.

'That was weird,' thought Fintan.

Maybe he should work on his friendly smile a bit?

SIX

Mrs Bongo was not a nice woman. In fact she was a thoroughly rotten one who had spent her whole life lying, stealing and hurting people. As a little girl she had stolen sweets, beaten up other children and stamped on their toys. As she grew up she had graduated to burgling people's houses, robbing people in the street, hijacking cars and generally being as rotten as possible.

At this moment in time Mrs Bongo was lurking behind a pillar in the lobby of the Hotel Impala, and listening very carefully to Lady Van der Kloot's conversation.

"Did you hear that?" she whispered to her equally rotten teenage son, "The old woman hasn't even got a safe!"

Her son, Suni, grinned stupidly. He couldn't help it, he was stupid.

"Yeah, Ma. It'll be so easy!" he chuckled displaying a frightening mess of teeth which stuck out like old gravestones.

"Come on, we need to make a plan," said Mrs Bongo waddling over to a seating area and slumping onto a comfy white sofa.

The woman was quite a peculiar sight. She had wild hair which stuck up at unexpected angles and an abnormally large bottom which made her look like she was smuggling watermelons in the back of her trousers.

"Right," she announced, leaning forward and talking in a secretive whisper, "First of all we're going need to steal a couple of hotel uniforms. I'll be a cook and you can be a cleaner. You get the old woman's room key, let yourself into her room and help yourself to the diamonds. No one will suspect a cleaner!"

Suni wasn't happy about this at all.

"But, Ma!" he whined, "I hate cleaning! Why can't I be a chef like you?"

"You don't actually have to do any cleaning, you idiot!" snapped his mother, "You just have to pretend!"

"But how come you get to be a chef?" continued Suni, "You're rubbish at cooking."

Mrs Bongo rolled her eyes, "I'm just pretending too, you moron!" she growled. "

"Well, can I be a porter then?" pleaded Suni, "I like those white uniforms. I'd look really smart in a white uniform."

His mother doubted this. Suni wouldn't look smart no matter what he was wearing.

"All right you can be a porter!" she hissed sounding very annoyed, "And when you've got the diamonds I'll take them to the kitchen and hide them in something so we can smuggle them out. Like inside a jar of jam or peanut butter or something."

"Or you could hide them up your nose maybe?" suggested Suni, "It's big enough!"

His mother glowered at him and kicked his shin under the coffee table. They were not nice people.

SEVEN

On the other side of the lobby Fintan had spotted another possible customer. This time it was a big, grubby man dressed entirely in camouflage clothing. He had a belt full of bullets strapped across his chest and a rifle slung over his shoulder. He looked just like one of the heroic African adventurers in Fintan's magazine.

The man stopped at the reception desk and dumped several grimy canvas bags on the floor. A shower of dust and mud fell onto the polished marble.

Feeling a little nervous, Fintan approached and had another go at his friendly smile.

"Can I carry your bags for you, sir?" he asked.

The man removed his sweat-stained hat and stared critically at him.

"What?" he snorted, apparently amused that this skinny little English boy thought he was capable of doing a grown man's work, "You want to carry my things?"

The man had such a strong South African accent that Fintan could barely understand what he was saying.

"I need to earn some money," admitted Fintan, nodding his head.

The man scratched something nasty out of his straggly beard and continued to eye Fintan thoughtfully.

"All right," he said eventually, "You've got yourself a job… if you think you can manage it. Don't expect any special treatment though. You'll be treated exactly the same as all my other bearers."

"Cool," said Fintan, "… What's a bearer?"

The man snorted again at Fintan's ignorance, "It means you get to carry my stuff, boy. Tents, food, water, that sort of thing. Load up the truck for me and I'll pay you five rand."

This sounded great! In fact it sounded like easy money. A few more customers like this and he'd soon have enough for the safari trip!

"OK," said Fintan happily.

Five minutes later it didn't look like quite such a good deal after all. The man's room was full of gear waiting to be loaded. There were about a hundred bags, boxes, trunks and cases, several enormous canvas tents with heavy wooden poles, camping stoves and cooking equipment, medicines, mosquito nets, water filtration equipment, and even a portable toilet. There was also a large number of guns and boxes of ammunition. All together it must have weighed a couple of tons!

"Henrik Bok," said the man extending a big damp hand.

Fintan looked blank. He didn't speak any foreign languages and was feeling a bit overwhelmed at the huge task he'd been given.

"It's my name, boy. I'm Henrik Bok."

"Oh right," said Fintan as his hand was crushed and shaken by the man's sweaty paw.

"Come and find me in the bar when you're done and you'll get your money, OK?"

For the next four and a half hours, Fintan carried every single item out of the hotel, dragged it across the car park and heaved it onto the back of the man's enormous truck. Well, almost every single item. There were a few that he lost on the way, a few more that he forgot to take and several others that he put in the wrong truck.

When he was finally finished he staggered back inside, aching all over and dripping with sweat. He found Mr Bok in the hotel bar lounging in a leather chair and sipping a large glass of whisky.

"All done," he said weakly.

Mr Bok was very drunk. He stared at Fintan with bloodshot eyes, struggling to remember who the exhausted looking boy was and what the thing was that he had just done.

"The truck," explained Fintan, "It's all loaded."

"Ah yes, the truck!" slurred Bok, rummaging in his pocket for a handful of coins, "What did we say? Two rand wasn't it?"

"Five, please," corrected Fintan.

Reluctantly the man paid up and returned to drinking his whisky.

"Thanks," said Fintan, "So where are you going? Are you going exploring?"

Bok nodded, "As soon as it's light we head into the bush. Big expedition," he mumbled.

"An expedition?" blurted Fintan excitedly, "Really? What are you looking for? I'm an explorer, too. Can I come?"

"No, you can't come," said Bok rudely, "And we're looking for big game."

Fintan wasn't sure what this meant. "Big game? What big game? Who's playing?"

Bok stared at him as if he was talking to an idiot "Big game, you domkop! Wild animals! I'm catching wild animals for a zoo."

He gestured towards the wall where the head of a water buffalo with massive curved horns had been stuffed and mounted.

"See that? I shot that one in the Karoo," he said proudly.

Fintan didn't know if the Karoo was a region of Africa or part of a buffalo. Either way, being shot in the Karoo didn't sound very pleasant.

"I don't like zoos," he said.

Fintan thought locking animals up in zoos was almost as bad as shooting them and sticking their heads on the wall. Zoos were like prisons for animals.

"Is that so? Well, who cares what you think!" sneered Bok, "Listen, boy, I'm catching animals for a zoo whether you like it or not, so clear off and leave me alone."

Fintan cleared off. He didn't like Mr. Bok. The man was rude, mean and cruel, and he smelled of sweaty armpits.

On the other hand, Fintan now had another five rand towards his safari trip which was good. He also had a new bag slung over his shoulder. It was a small canvas one belonging to Mr Bok which he had accidentally walked off with. Neither of them had noticed it due to Bok being very drunk and Fintan being very tired and… well…very Fintan. It was an important bag, too, containing important things. Mr. Bok was going to find it difficult to shoot any animals without his tranquilliser darts.

EIGHT

It was the end of a rotten day. Fintan had worked for eighteen hours and only had ten rand to show for it. It wasn't enough.

As he shuffled towards his room he noticed the hotel's kitchen door was half open. Even though it was about three in the morning a bright light was coming from inside. A vague idea formed in his soggy brain. Maybe there were some kitchen jobs he could do, like washing up or peeling potatoes. It was certainly worth asking.

"Excuse me," he called, pushing open the kitchen door a little and peering inside, "Is anybody here?"

There was no reply but he could hear hushed voices and clinking sounds coming from a small store room at the back. Very carefully, he walked through the deserted kitchen, edging past several stacks of saucepans, plates and prepared vegetables. Knocking something over now might spoil his chances of getting a job.

In the storeroom he came across two African hotel workers standing with their backs to him. One was a boy of about his own age wearing a smart, white porter's uniform. He appeared to be jabbing at something shiny with a potato peeler. The other, a woman with an abnormally large bottom, dressed as a chef, was stuffing tiny things into a jar. Both of them were in a big hurry and looked very excited.

"Hello," said Fintan, "Sorry to disturb you, but are there any kitchen jobs going?"

For some reason both of them leapt up in fright and tried to hide what they were doing.

"Get out!" hissed the chef, "You can't come in here!"

"Sorry," said Fintan, "The door was open and… are there any jobs going? I'm not fussy. I'll do the washing up if you like… or peel the spuds or something?"

He took the potato peeler from the boy's hand to demonstrate how skilled he was and jabbed it in a mango several times. They didn't seem very impressed.

"No! No jobs!" said the African boy looking very flustered and shoving Fintan back towards the door, "Go away!"

Fintan thought this was a bit rude. He was only looking for work after all. There was no need for shouting and pushing! Then he caught a glimpse of what they were trying to hide from him. It appeared to be a large jar full of something brown and creamy.

"Wait… is that peanut butter?" he asked, immediately forgetting about the job, "I haven't seen that sort before. Is it a South African one?"

"None of your business, boy!" said the lumpy chef, standing in front of it protectively.

Fintan loved peanut butter. His ambition was to try every brand in the world so this was an opportunity not to miss!

"Can't I just have a little bit?" he said, fumbling in his pocket for his ten rand, "I've got some money, look."

The skinny porter boy pushed Fintan's hand aside, "Not for sale!" he snapped.

"Just enough for one sandwich?" spluttered Fintan, wondering why the boy's arm was now wrapped around his throat.

"Go away. There is nothing for you here!" added the chef, joining in the struggle and pushing him as hard as she could.

Fintan couldn't understand why they were reacting like this. It seemed a bit extreme! South African peanut butter must be pretty special if hotel staff were prepared to fight him for it! Suddenly the chef leapt back as if she'd been stung by a bee.

"Ow!" she yelped, "What have you got in your bag?"

This confused Fintan even more.

"What bag?" he said.

He spun around and discovered a brown canvas bag slung over his shoulder. This was very odd. It hadn't been there earlier. It must be one of Mr Bok's.

Even more confusingly the chef was now staggering backwards across the storeroom with her eyes all glassy. She stumbled, thumped face-first into a wall and collapsed heavily to the floor.

"What did you do to my mother?" gasped the youth staring down at the unconscious chef in disbelief.

"I don't know," said Fintan, peering into the bag, "Maybe there's something—"

Before he could finish his sentence the porter had jumped on him and knocked him over. For the next couple of minutes they flailed around on the storeroom floor like a bundle of angry laundry. There was a flurry of fists and bony kneecaps as they banged into cupboards causing an avalanche of carrots, cabbages and tinned fruit. Then, very abruptly, the fighting stopped. Fintan lay on his back gazing right up the African boy's cavernous nostrils. For some reason his adversary had gone very quiet and wasn't moving. Even when a dozen tins of peas fell on the back of his head he just lay there and didn't react. Something weird was going on. Both the chef and now the young porter had suddenly passed out.

Fintan disentangled himself from the unconscious boy and stood up, brushing bits of squashed vegetable from his clothes. The storeroom looked like a hurricane had blown through it. Almost everything had been knocked over or broken and, worse still, there was a chef and a hotel porter lying on the floor, open mouthed and drooling. Fintan had no idea what had happened to them. He had another peek into Mr Bok's bag and immediately found the answer. It was full of tranquilliser darts. Hundreds of them rolled into tight bundles and intended for knocking out wild animals. The chef and the porter had probably been jabbed with a big enough dose to incapacitate a water buffalo! They wouldn't be waking up for hours.

Fintan decided he should probably go before he got into trouble. As he picked his way out through the mess of dented tins and broken glass he noticed something miraculous: one of the jars of peanut butter which had fallen to the floor hadn't smashed at all. It was the only survivor! Smiling to himself he picked it up and popped it into his new canvas bag. He would need some bread to go with it, of course, so he helped himself to half a very squashed loaf which had been kicked around on the floor.

After this he piled all his tip money on a worktop as payment and wrote a quick thank you note on the kitchen chalkboard. It would have been rude not to.

NINE

When Fintan finally got back to his room it was approaching dawn. He tiptoed across the carpet taking care not to wake his horrible brother who was lying face down and snoring like a wounded moose. Judging by the state Flavian's back, the idiot must have spent the whole day in the African sun. He looked as if he had been boiled. His whole back, neck and shoulders were as red and shiny as strawberry jelly and seemed to be glowing in the dark.

Fintan sat on his creaky camp-bed and rubbed his eyes. He was exhausted, broke and covered in bruises and bits of cabbage but there was still something important he had to do before going to sleep. Very carefully he opened Bok's canvas bag and, avoiding the bundles of tranquilliser darts, took out the bread and the extremely large, unbroken jar. The label said 'White Lion Peanut Butter' and had an exciting picture of a roaring lion with a shaggy, white mane. It looked great. He got out his pen knife, cut the loaf into large chunky slices and spread a thick peanut buttery layer over the whole lot. It was delicious! Different though. South African peanut butter was a lot crunchier than the English stuff. In fact some bites were so crunchy he almost broke a tooth and had to swallow it without chewing. Three sandwiches later he was stuffed. He climbed under his bedcovers, completely worn out but happy.

What he didn't know was that he had just eaten a million rands worth of tiny diamonds.

TEN

Just before dawn, Mrs Bongo and Suni regained consciousness. They found themselves lying on the storeroom floor surrounded by bits of food, tins of peas and several smashed jars. And they were not happy at all. Their heads were throbbing and their bodies felt like they had been trampled by an angry elephant. But worse still, their jar of peanut butter had gone. The one they had just hidden the diamonds in!

"It has to be here somewhere!" moaned Suni, checking beneath the cupboards for the third time, "Are you sure it's missing, Ma?"

"Of course I'm sure!" snapped his mother, with her hands on her wide hips, "Shut up and keep looking, boy."

For the next two miserable hours they crawled on their hands and knees, peering under cookers, reaching down drains and rummaging through bins. The real kitchen staff would be arriving for work soon so there wasn't much time left. Still there was no sign of the missing jar. Mrs Bongo stood up, aching and fuming.

"Wait… what's that?" she said pointing at a blackboard on the wall.

The blackboard was normally used for writing down dinner orders but someone had scribbled a message on it. Together they hurried over for a closer look. The message read:

'*Took bread and peanut butter. Here is money. Thanks.*'

Below it on the kitchen work top was a handful of coins. They added up to exactly ten rand.

"I knew it!" raged Mrs Bongo, snatching up a damp rag and wiping the blackboard clean. "I knew it was that English boy!"

"The rotten thief!" said her son, even though he was a rotten thief himself, "D'you think he knew there were diamonds in it, Ma? Maybe he just wanted the peanut butter like he said? Maybe it was just a coincidence?"

"A coincidence?" sneered Mrs Bongo, "Don't be stupid! Think about it. Why would he wander into the kitchen in the middle of the night looking for a job? How unlikely is that? And what is the *only* thing he takes? The jar with the diamonds in!"

"And half a loaf of bread," added Suni a bit weakly.

"It was *no* coincidence," snarled the pretend chef grabbing her son by the arm and heading for the door, "He knew *exactly* what he was doing. He was stealing our diamonds!"

She paused a moment at a rack full of kitchen knives and selected a huge, sharp meat cleaver.

"And we're going to get them back!"

ELEVEN

Fintan was exhausted. After such a busy day and late night, he had been hoping for a nice lie-in but unfortunately he didn't get one. Just before six o'clock a piercing scream woke up the whole hotel. It was Lady Van der Kloot. She came hurrying down to the lobby as fast as her creaky old legs and fluffy slippers would allow.

"I've been robbed!" she screeched, "My diamonds are gone! Someone call the police at once!"

The hotel receptionist leapt into action. There was a lot of activity, some frantic phone calls and some shouting. Within half an hour a police inspector had arrived and all the hotel's guests had been woken and gathered in the lobby.

The policeman, a tall, serious-looking African man, wearing a beige suit and a small grey moustache called for everyone to be silent. Fintan immediately let out an enormous yawn and his stomach made an odd grumbling noise.

"Pardon," he said.

"My name is Inspector Kudubenikubiza of the South African Police," began the policeman, "But you may call me Inspector Kudu."

'That's a relief,' thought Fintan.

"I have gathered you all here because a serious crime has been committed in this hotel. A valuable piece of diamond jewellery has been stolen from a guest and it is possible that one of you is the thief."

A hushed murmur spread through the crowd.

"I will be interviewing you one by one. Please be patient and we'll have this over as soon as possible."

Everyone groaned. They had made plans! They had safaris to go on and seminars on cake marketing to attend. Gribley had a pile of ironing to do and Felicity and Flavian were going to be late for their sunbathing! Speaking of which, where was Flavian? Fintan looked all around the crowd but there was no sign of him. The lazy bum must have stayed in bed!

TWELVE

At that moment the lazy bum, Flavian, was awoken by a
noise. Someone was banging about in his room,
rummaging through his things and throwing them about.
Naturally, he assumed it was his annoying little brother. It
usually was but this time it was different.

"Shut up, Fintan, you idiot!" he muttered without
raising his head from the pillow, "I'm trying to sleep
here!"

The noise continued anyway. Flavian sighed heavily,
groped around on the floor and picked up a shoe to
throw.

"I'm warning you, little brother!" he said, "Shut up or
I'll—"

Suddenly someone with an abnormally large bottom
sat down heavily on his sunburnt back. Flavian opened
his mouth to scream but a hand reached down and closed
it again.

"Be quiet, boy!" said an African woman's voice, "Tell us where you put it and you won't get hurt."

It was too late for that, thought Flavian. It was already hurting. A lot!

"Get off me!" he squealed through the stranger's fingers, "I don't know what you're talking about! Honestly I don't!"

"Liar! We know you took it," hissed another voice from the other side of the room.

It sounded as if someone was tipping things out of drawers and scattering them around. Both strangers sounded very African and very scary.

"Do you want money?" continued Flavian in a strange whimper, "I've got money if you want it! My dad's loaded!"

There was a clatter as the rubbish bin was tipped out and the peanut butter jar hit the floor.

"It's here, I found it!" said an excited voice, "But it's empty!"

Anyone who knew Fintan wouldn't have been surprised by this. He never wasted peanut butter and had eaten every last bit of it... including the million rands worth of diamonds.

The woman with the large bottom was furious. She raised her huge meat cleaver then slammed it down onto the bed. It sliced right through Flavian's pillow a few inches from his nose.

"Where are they? Where did you put them?" she demanded.

Flavian squealed as bits of feather stuffing flew into the air and up his nostrils, "What do you...? What? I don't... I... pardon?" he bleated.

He really did have no idea what she was talking about.

The woman leaned in closely and spoke right into his ear, "Tell us where they are or I'll—"

"Wait, Ma!" interrupted Suni, staring oddly at Flavian's terrified face, "This is not the right boy. This boy is too big."

The African woman stood up and stared at him, too. He was definitely bigger than the boy they were looking for. And much redder.

"Where's the other boy?" she insisted.

"What other boy?" asked Flavian then suddenly understood what was happening, "Wait... are you looking for my little brother? Scruffy haired boy? Always getting into trouble? Sort of an idiot? He's in that camp bed over there by the door!"

The intruders glanced at the camp bed. It was empty apart from a tangled mess of sheets and breadcrumbs. They had missed him. He was probably downstairs already. The woman retrieved her meat cleaver from the pillow and leaned in closely again.

"We'll be watching you!" she hissed then left the room, muttering and cursing in her own language.

Flavian didn't understand a word of it but he could tell it was something pretty scary. For a while he lay completely still in a state of shock. His heart was beating like a steam pump and his sunburnt back was stinging. Terrified, he scrambled out of bed and hid underneath it. He didn't like Africa anymore.

THIRTEEN

Lady Van der Kloot had been given a chair right next to the Police Inspector while he made his announcements. She was sitting there looking distraught and fanning herself.

"Thank you, Inspector," she said, when he had finished speaking, "May I just add that the tiara was a gift to me from my late husband which means it has great sentimental value. It is also worth a small fortune! Therefore I have decided to offer a small reward of five thousand rand for its safe return."

Another murmur ran through the crowd, an excited one this time. Fintan's mouth fell open. He was so tired he could barely stand up but this had really caught his attention.

Five thousand rand? He had no idea how many pounds that was but it sounded like a lot of money! Easily enough for a safari trip and some left over to pay his dad back for all the damage!

"Did you hear that, Gribs!" he whispered, nudging his butler's arm, "That's a fortune! Maybe I should do a bit of detective work of my own!"

He rubbed his chin and narrowed his eyes like detectives did in movies. One of the people in the lobby was probably the diamond thief! He cast an eye over the assembled crowd to see if any of them looked a bit dodgy. Could it be one of the podgy business people? Maybe one of them was actually an international diamond thief, just pretending to be there for the cake conference? Unfortunately none of them looked particularly guilty or was wearing an eye-mask and stripy shirt like robbers did in cartoons. Being a detective wasn't easy. Maybe the dull family from Croydon who moaned a lot were only *pretending* to be a dull family from Croydon who moaned a lot but were actually hardened criminals? Perhaps one of the hotel staff had done it? The receptionist had certainly known about the diamonds and had put the old lady in a room with no safe. Or maybe Lady Van der Kloot was making it all up? Maybe she was just pretending her diamonds had been stolen to claim the insurance money? Were those real tears in her eyes or was it all just a cunning trick?

Finally Fintan's gaze settled on Henrik Bok, the big game hunter. Now *there* was a shifty looking man! He was standing at the back of the crowd with his arms folded, leaning on the wall and looking impatient to leave. Exactly the sort of behaviour you'd expect from a rotten, guilt-ridden diamond thief! There was now no doubt in Fintan's mind who had done it.

FOURTEEN

One by one, the police interviewed all the guests and staff in the Hotel Impala, hoping to find the diamond thief. Well, all the guests except Flavian, of course, who was hiding under his bed, and all the staff except Mrs Bongo and Suni who didn't actually work there and were hiding in the toilet until the police had gone. Eventually, it was Fintan's turn to be seen. He was escorted into the hotel manager's office where he was photographed, fingerprinted and searched by an assortment of police officers. After this he was taken to a small room and seated opposite a very stern-looking Inspector Kudu.

"Right then, sonny," began the inspector, "What is your full name."

Fintan yawned noisily, struggling to stay awake. "It's Fintan, your honour."

"Your *full* name, please. And you don't have to call me your honour."

"Full name, right. It's Fintan Columbus Livingstone Shackleton Fedora. Aged fourteen and a half, your highness." It wasn't really his name but he'd often wished it was. His middle name was Norman.

The inspector peered at him over his glasses but didn't react.

"And why are you here?"

"Holiday," said Fintan, then quickly changed his mind, "Actually, no. Not really. Well, not a *proper* holiday anyway. I'm supposed to be here for the cake conference. I'm not going to it or anything but Auntie Fiona wouldn't let me go to her place again because I made her poodle go a bit blue. It was an accident. Making the poodle go blue. I didn't mean it."

Inspector Kudu reluctantly wrote it all down.

"Oh, and I'm also here to get a job," added Fintan.

The inspector nodded and added it to his notes.

"What were your movements last night between 9 PM and five AM?" he asked.

"My movements?" said Fintan.

"It means where were you?" said the inspector.

"Oh right! Well, er… I was in the lobby for a bit. Did quite a lot of moving about in there. Then at about three in the morning I went to the kitchen and after that I went to bed."

Inspector Kudu suddenly looked very interested.

"The kitchen, you say? Why did you go there?"

"I was trying to get a job," said Fintan proudly, "Look, it says so here…"

He pointed helpfully at the inspector's notebook.

"At three o'clock in the morning?"

Fintan nodded, "Yep. But they said they didn't have any jobs."

He decided not to mention the little incident with the peanut butter, the fighting and knocking the hotel staff unconscious. He didn't want to get into trouble.

"I see," continued the inspector, even though he was beginning to think the boy was a bit insane, "And did you notice anything suspicious at all? Anyone behaving strangely?"

Fintan thought about this for a while, stared at the ceiling and drummed his fingers on his knees.

"Well, I saw that big game hunter man, Mr Bok, loitering around. Does that count?"

The inspector said nothing but wrote it down anyway.

"I bet *he* did it," said Fintan.

FIFTEEN

The following day Gribley came down to breakfast with three tickets for the balloon safari but unfortunately Flavian didn't want to go anymore. For reasons no one could fully understand he was hiding under his bed and refusing to come out. His room was a terrible mess but everyone just assumed it was Fintan's fault. All Flavian would say was that he didn't like Africa anymore and he wanted to go home. His parents, his sister and Gribley had all tried to persuade him to come out and talk about it but he wouldn't move. It was very peculiar. Fintan, on the other hand, thought it was a stroke of luck.

"Can I have his safari ticket then?" he suggested.

The family thought this was very inconsiderate, taking advantage of poor Flavian's problems, but they couldn't come up with a good reason why he shouldn't.

An hour later a large 4x4 vehicle painted with zebra stripes arrived at the hotel to pick them up. It was big and shiny and had Luxafari written on it in big gold letters. Gribley climbed in followed by Felicity, who was clutching her glossy leaflet and thinking about the gorgeous balloon pilot. She had dressed herself up in her best sparkly dress and matching high-heeled shoes. It wasn't exactly safari clothing but, then again, she wasn't exactly going to see the animals. There was no sign of Fintan.

This wasn't unusual. The boy rarely turned up on time for anything and often didn't turn up at all. Eventually Gribley went and found him on the other side of the hotel waiting in the wrong car park.

"What've you got in there, moron boy?" sneered Felicity as Fintan arrived carrying a surprisingly large backpack, "We're only going for a couple of hours, not a week!"

Her own bag was surprisingly big, too. It contained three changes of clothes, several different ranges of cosmetics, two hair driers and some hair straighteners, even though there was nowhere to plug them in, and some glossy magazines in case she got bored.

"It's my survival kit," mumbled Fintan, "In case of emergency."

"Survival kit?" snorted his sister, "OMG, you're such a little freak! Isn't he a freak, Gribs?"

Gribley didn't answer. The car drove off and Felicity continued moaning.

"And what on earth are you wearing? Those clothes are *so* stupid looking! No one wears khaki any more. It's *so* last season!"

Fintan frowned. He was wearing sensible safari clothes and boots which didn't have high-heels. His sister was stupid.

"And will you do us all a favour and lose that ridiculous floppy hat? It's totally hideous. You can't possibly go out looking like that! Tell him, Gribley! Tell him to change. He's *so* embarrassing!"

Gribley dared to disagree. He politely suggested that if anyone's choice of clothing might be a bit impractical it was Felicity's. Felicity was furious and shrieked a lot. Fintan informed his sister that his survival kit was recommended by *Young Adventurer* magazine and that they ought to know what they were talking about. Felicity demanded that her younger brother stay away from her for the rest of the day and under no circumstances tell the pilot they were related. The driver, who was one of South Africa's Xhosa people, didn't speak any English at all, which was unfortunate for him as he really wanted to tell them to shut up. All the bad tempered shouting was giving him a headache.

The car made its way out of the city and into the African bush. It was Fintan's first glimpse of the real Africa and he loved it. Low rocky hills covered in dry, brown grass and scrubby trees, all baking beneath a vivid blue sky and a hot African sun. What none of them noticed, however, was that they were being followed. Two weird-looking African people on bicycles were pedalling furiously along a short distance behind. One of them had an unnaturally large bottom.

SIXTEEN

When they reached the launch site the hot air balloon was waiting for them, almost fully inflated. It was an enormous royal blue thing with Luxafari written on it in gold letters. The handsome pilot was already in the basket making some final adjustments to the burners. Felicity took a little mirror from her purse and checked her make-up.

"Don't you dare spoil this for me," she snarled, giving her brother an evil stare.

"Spoil what?" said Fintan.

He was far too excited to let his silly sister bother him. He had never been in a hot air balloon before and couldn't wait. Even if it was called 'Luxafari' and had fancy snacks and champagne on board it was the nearest thing to adventure he had seen in ages.

The pilot, a tall Zulu man, welcomed everyone with his perfect white smile and escorted them to the balloon basket. Unlike the driver, he spoke perfect English and was dressed in a crisply pressed white shirt and black tie. Felicity thought he looked very heroic. She also thought he was even better-looking in real life than he was in his photo and had to fan herself with the glossy brochure to avoid fainting.

It was surprisingly spacious inside the balloon basket and felt very sturdy. The pilot calmly explained that the safari would follow the wind which was currently blowing in a north-westerly direction. It would take them out over the immense African plains and should offer spectacular views of wildlife. Towards evening they would land and be met by the recovery vehicle then enjoy a luxury sunset supper and a glass of chilled champagne. He also reassured Felicity that she was very unlikely to step in any dung.

Felicity sighed happily. It all sounded very romantic and very classy. She gazed lovingly at the pilot, told him he must be very brave and giggled a lot.

Fintan thought it all sounded a bit stupid. Champagne and caviar on a safari! That was about as soppy as you could get!

The handsome pilot pulled a metal lever above his head, sending jets of flaming hot air up into the balloon.

There was an exciting roaring noise and the whole basket vibrated slightly. They were ready for takeoff.

However, just as they were about to depart, the pilot spotted a problem. Two furious looking African people had turned up on bicycles and were trying to push their way past the driver of the recovery vehicle. It was quickly turning into a very heated argument. The younger of the two angry Africans, a skinny youth with buck teeth, was sneering nastily and looking very aggressive, while the older one, a woman with a large bottom was yelling and pointing towards the balloon.

Fintan thought they looked oddly familiar. They weren't wearing their hotel uniforms anymore but it was definitely the people he had met in the kitchen. The woman's enormous bottom was unmistakable. But what were they doing there? Maybe they wanted to go on a balloon safari too?

"Excuse me a moment, please," said the pilot sounding very calm, professional and handsome.

He climbed out of the basket and hurried over to see what was going on. Things immediately got even worse. The big woman produced a meat cleaver and began waving it around in a threatening way.

"What's happening?" said Felicity, cowering behind her butler, "Who are those frightful people?"

"They work at the hotel," said Fintan, "They're a bit nuts, if you ask me."

As he spoke Suni thumped the driver in the face so hard that the poor man dropped senseless to the ground. Whatever it was they wanted, it probably wasn't a safari.

Mrs Bongo shoved the pilot aside and charged towards the balloon.

"You, boy!" she yelled pointing furiously at Fintan.

She reached into the basket and grabbed Fintan by his shirt collar.

"Typical!" tutted Felicity, glaring at her little brother, "I should have known it would all be *his* fault!"

"Give them back!" screamed Mrs Bongo, "We know you've got them!"

Fintan felt himself being shaken around like a doll in a bulldog's mouth.

"Pardon?" he said innocently, "Are you talking about the peanut butter?"

"Yeah! And the half a loaf of bread!" added Suni, missing the point again.

Fintan couldn't believe they were still angry about something so unimportant. It was only a jar of peanut butter after all! And he'd paid for it, too!

"But… I ate it," he said.

"You ate it?" shrieked Mrs Bongo in disbelief, "What, all of it?"

Fintan nodded, thinking it was a daft question. What else was he supposed to do with a jar of peanut butter? Take it for a walk?

Mrs Bongo stared into Fintan's confused looking face and got the strange impression that he might actually be telling the truth! It seemed unlikely but perhaps he hadn't known the jar was stuffed with priceless diamonds at all! Maybe he had known nothing about it and just eaten them by mistake. The boy wasn't a thief after all. He was just some daft English kid with a peculiar interest in trying different brands of peanut butter!

"So… it's in your belly now?" she mused, lowering the cleaver to his stomach and circling it around menacingly.

Fintan thought for a moment then nodded again. His visits to the loo were usually as regular as clockwork but for some reason he hadn't been that morning. It was probably all the fancy hotel food he'd been eating. Either that or the whole jar of peanut butter he'd swallowed the night before.

"Must be," he said.

Mrs Bongo grinned insanely, "Well in that case, boy," she snarled, "I'm going to have to open you up like a fish!"

"Excuse me, Madam," interrupted Gribley, deciding things were getting out of hand, "I'm sure there's no need for that. There's obviously been some sort of misunderstanding."

Mrs Bongo didn't even look up. She let go of Fintan's collar for a moment and punched Gribley right between the eyes. He fell backwards like a dropped sack of potatoes and landed heavily on Fintan's backpack. Felicity screamed and tried unsuccessfully to climb out of the basket. Mrs Bongo returned her attention to Fintan and the important business of getting the stolen diamonds back. Fintan thought she must be completely mad. Who on earth would want to cut someone open to retrieve some half-digested peanut butter? Especially when there was plenty more of it available in the local supermarket which hadn't already been swallowed!

"What if I bought you a replacement jar?" suggested Fintan as the demented woman raised her cleaver and prepared to start slicing, "Or two jars if you like? I don't mind, honest!"

At that moment the handsome pilot grabbed Mrs Bongo's wrist and tried to force her to drop her weapon but she was gripping it really tightly. Seconds later Suni leapt onto the pilot's back and sank his teeth into his handsome left ear. The pilot screamed. There was a lot of pushing and shoving and kicking and hair pulling which rocked the balloon basket violently. Fintan broke free and took a step backwards.

"I want my diamonds!" screeched Mrs Bongo, wild-eyed and furious. She swung her cleaver around in huge dangerous swipes, narrowly missing Fintan's head but cutting through a thick rope. The balloon jerked upwards throwing everyone about. Mrs Bongo had severed the mooring cable which was the only thing holding the balloon on the ground. A sudden urgency gripped her. The boy was getting away and so were her diamonds! Clenching her cleaver between her teeth, she grabbed onto the rapidly rising basket and was lifted swiftly off her feet. She swung one leg up and tried to hook her stinky shoe over the top edge but couldn't quite find the strength to pull herself up. The balloon rose a few more metres and was tugged sideways by a small gust of wind. Mrs Bongo couldn't hold on any longer. She lost her grip and plummeted bottom-first onto the handsome pilot's head, pinning him to the ground beneath her massive buttocks. There was a terrible cracking sound as his lower jaw twisted round to the side of his head. The pain brought tears to his eyes.

"Oh my God, what have you done, Fintan?" squealed Felicity, looking over the side, "You've left the pilot behind! You absolute idiot!"

"Me?" protested Fintan, "I didn't do it! It was that old woman that cut the rope, not me!"

"Oh shut up and *do* something will you!" yelled Felicity, wild-eyed with panic, "We're getting higher all the time!"

Both of them turned expectantly to Gribley. He was older, wiser and more experienced. He was always sensible and calm in a crisis and experienced in all sorts of useful things. He would know what to do. Unfortunately Gribley was slumped in the corner of the basket on Fintan's bag. There was a strange, vacant expression on his face.

"I wouldn't sit on that if I were you, Gribs," cautioned Fintan, "It's got a load of tranquilliser darts in it."

Felicity screamed again and pummelled her brother with punches.

"Make it stop, you little idiot! I want to go back down!"

Fintan looked around with absolutely no idea how he was supposed to stop the balloon rising. He had seen how the pilot made it go higher by shooting hot air from the burner but that was the opposite of what he wanted.

There were a few heavy sandbags strapped to the side of the basket which he was pretty sure had something to do with making it go down… or possibly up. He wasn't sure. Hurriedly he untied one and heaved it over the side. It landed on the handsome pilot's already painful head causing him to howl in agony. The balloon rose even faster, so that wasn't the solution.

He noticed a coil of rope with a metal hook on the end. It looked like some sort of anchor which was obviously meant to attach to something but he had no idea what. He lobbed it over the side towards a small clump of trees hoping to snag something solid like a branch or a root but it just thumped onto the dusty earth. He peered down watching the four African people below grow smaller and smaller. Two of them were looking up and shaking their furious fists at him while one was crouching on the ground nursing a broken jaw and the other was lying flat on his back, totally senseless. The balloon was going whether Felicity liked it or not.

Moments later the anchor rope pulled tight. It had attached to something after all. Unfortunately for Fintan it hadn't attached to something heavy enough to hold the balloon down. And unfortunately for Suni it had attached to the belt loop on the back of his trousers.

SEVENTEEN

Back at the hotel, Inspector Kudu was kneeling on the floor of Flavian's room and peering under the bed.

"Look, I'm not coming out and that's final," insisted Flavian, "It's not safe out there."

He had been refusing to cooperate for at least ten minutes now, which was a pity because he was the only person in the whole hotel with any useful information about the diamond thieves. The Inspector was becoming more and more annoyed. His knees were aching, too.

"All right," sighed Kudu, "You can stay under there if you like, but you really must try to answer my questions. Do you understand?"

There was a long pause while Flavian appeared to be considering the proposal.

"I want to go home," he whined eventually, pulling another blanket under the bed with him.

Kudu wasn't ready to give up just yet, "OK, boy, tell me what happened in here then," he said, glancing around at the messy bedroom, "Why is your room in such a terrible mess?"

It looked as if it had been attacked by a troop of angry baboons. Furniture had been tipped over, all the drawers had been emptied out onto the floor, the wastepaper bin had been upended and some of the bedding had been ripped apart with a sharp implement.

"Tell me the truth now, who did this?"

"I don't want to talk about it," whimpered Flavian, hiding behind his protective blanket.

"Was it anything to do with your younger brother?"

Flavian made a sudden jerking movement and banged his head on the bottom of the bed.

"Ow!" he barked, sounding angry and terrified at the same time, "Well, it usually is, isn't it!"

It was an extreme reaction and one which Inspector Kudu found very interesting. He had been hearing quite a lot about young Fintan Fedora lately. No one seemed to like him or trust him. Even the boy's brother, sister and parents had found it hard to say anything nice about him. He looked harmless enough and was certainly no criminal mastermind but somehow all the evidence was pointing towards him being involved in the diamond theft.

Fintan's name had come up again and again during Kudu's interviews with the hotel guests. Many of them had reported suspicious incidents involving a scruffy little English boy. Several guests said he had tried to get money from them by carrying their bags even though he didn't work there. Lady Van der Kloot had said the boy even tried to take her purse full of valuables out of her hands. Mr Bok, the big game hunter, had mentioned trusting the boy with his bags only to find that several of them went missing and that despite this the boy had also demanded money from him. The hotel's kitchen staff had said some very interesting things during their interviews, too. It turned out that none of them had been approached by a boy asking for a job and that no one worked in the kitchen during the night anyway; which meant that Fintan had made it up. But why would he do that?

Kudu stood up and rubbed his aching knees. He turned to his sergeant who was busy searching through the disastrous mess and putting various suspicious items into plastic bags.

"Just found this, sir," said the sergeant, holding up a crumpled porter's jacket, "The boy must have disguised himself as a porter so he could sneak into Lady Van der Kloot's room."

Actually, Suni had dumped it there after ransacking the room, but to the police it was yet more evidence of Fintan's guilt. It really wasn't looking good for the boy. He was rapidly becoming Inspector Kudu's prime suspect.

There was a knock at the door and two more uniformed policemen came in wearing rubber gloves and revolted expressions. They had just finished the unpleasant task of searching through all the bins and drains in the kitchen.

"Excuse me, Inspector Kudu, sir," said one, "But you need to see this."

He handed over a plastic evidence bag containing Lady Van der Kloot's missing tiara. All the diamonds had been wrenched out with some sort of metal tool.

"We found it hidden at the bottom of a plastic bucket full of food waste, sir," said the policeman looking as if he was going to be sick, "Very stinky it was."

"Found this in there, too, Inspector," added the other policeman holding up another clear plastic bag.

It contained a potato peeler with a very bent tip.

"Exactly the sort of metal tool which might have been used to dig the diamonds out of the tiara, sir... and it's covered in Fintan Fedora's fingerprints."

EIGHTEEN

The view from the hot air balloon was stunningly fabulous. An enormous expanse of reddish brown earth dotted with acacia trees stretching all the way to a distant blue horizon. Vast herds of antelope and zebra ambled casually about while hippos and crocodiles lay half-submerged in muddy brown pools. Fintan thought it was brilliant.

It was just a shame that Gribley was missing it all. He would have really enjoyed it. Unfortunately the poor man was completely comatose with a bottom full of tranquilliser darts. Felicity was squatting next to him with her head in her hands, muttering murderous things to herself. Fintan decided it was safer not to try talking to her.

He peered over the side of the basket to see what had happened to the pilot. Way below them, bumping over the dusty ground, Fintan could see the recovery vehicle following behind. This meant the driver must be OK and would still be able to pick them up when they landed. He could also hear some faint shouts but couldn't make out what was being said. He presumed it was the pilot trying to tell him what to do.

But it wasn't. The pilot was still back at the launch site nursing his broken jaw and the driver was still flat on his back. The recovery vehicle was, in fact, being driven by a very angry Mrs Bongo who didn't really know how to drive which is why it was weaving madly all over the place. The weird shouts, meanwhile, were coming from her skinny son, Suni who was dangling beneath the balloon on the end of the rope.

Another desperate yell came from somewhere below which sounded quite urgent. Fintan looked ahead and noticed a clump of tall trees. The pilot must be telling him to gain a bit of height he thought. He pulled the lever, just as he had seen the pilot do, and sent more hot air up into the balloon. The burners roared, blue flames shot up and the balloon rose several more metres into the air. The basket cleared the tops of the branches by a few centimetres. It was such a perfect, skilful manoeuvre, especially for a beginner, that Fintan couldn't help feeling pretty proud of himself. What he couldn't understand was why it was followed by such loud screams and scraping noises from below.

NINETEEN

Unlike Fintan, Suni was not enjoying his first ever balloon ride. Being dragged through a thorn tree while dangling from your trouser belt loop is not a pleasant experience. Especially when you're 20 metres above the ground and don't particularly like heights.

"Ma!" he yelled, picking spiky twigs out of his torn clothes, "Help! Get me down! I don't like it!"

Unfortunately there was very little Mrs Bongo could do. Her son was just too high to reach and anyway, she was busy trying to steer the 4x4 over the rutted ground and avoid the rock-hard termite mounds. She would just have to keep following the balloon until it ran out of fuel and came back down to earth. And when it did, that English boy was going to be in serious trouble!

TWENTY

Five hours went by and the balloon continued to drift with the wind. Fintan continued to enjoy himself enormously, Felicity continued sulking and Gribley continued to lie motionless in the corner. Occasionally they would rise to a hundred metres or so where the air was much chillier but most of the time they sailed along quite close to the ground. On a couple of occasions when they got a bit too low, Fintan had released one of the many ballast sandbags tied onto the side of the basket. Only one of them hit the recovery vehicle though. He had shouted down to say he was sorry for breaking the windscreen but wasn't sure if anyone had heard.

A little later, Fintan was enjoying the incredible view when he spotted a group of people below. He could see they were creeping stealthily through the tall grass towards a large herd of zebra. Fintan realised the man at the front with the gun must be Mr Bok. It was a shame but he appeared to have found some more tranquilliser darts to shoot animals with.

"Hello!" Shouted Fintan, "Hello, Mr Bok. It's me!"

No one looked up. The balloon was obviously much too high for his voice to be heard. However, a quick noisy blast of hot air from the burner got the hunter's attention. It also got the attention of the herd of zebra which immediately ran away. Mr Bok stared up furiously and shook his fist.

"Moron!" he muttered through clenched teeth, "We're miles from civilisation and *still* there's some idiot in a balloon who manages to ruin my hunt!"

Seconds later there was the roar of an engine and the recovery vehicle came crashing through the long grass. It bounced over the rutted ground and blundered through termite mounds. Bok shrieked in terror as it thundered right at him. He dived out of the way and landed painfully on the rock-hard ground.

Suni, meanwhile, spent the day gathering more spikes, thorns and broken branches in his hair as well as an impressive collection of scratches and bruises. At one point he was dunked in a lake full of snapping crocodiles which at least washed most of the rubbish out of his clothes. There was also an unfortunate collision with a giraffe which was so annoyed at being thumped into that it bit Suni in the leg.

Finally, Mrs Bongo managed to steer the battered truck right under the balloon just in time for her son to be dumped onto the roof rack. Suni held on desperately while his mother passed him her meat cleaver through the broken windscreen. It took several swings of the cleaver but eventually he chopped through the rope and was free.

"We did it, Ma!" he yelled triumphantly, "We did it!"

His mother gripped the steering wheel furiously and glared at the balloon above them, "Of course we did!" she barked, "Now we just need to catch that interfering b—"

The rest of her sentence was cut off as she drove over the edge of a cliff.

TWENTY ONE

Gribley regained consciousness to find himself lying upside down in a tree. He had no idea how he had got there.

"Oh, hello, Gribs," said a surprisingly cheerful Fintan who was sitting on the next branch whittling a stick with his penknife, "Are you feeling better now?"

Gribley didn't know. His head was throbbing, he had a terrible thirst and his bottom felt like he had been sitting on a beanbag stuffed with hedgehogs.

"Where are we, sir?" he croaked, trying to turn himself the right way up, "What on earth just happened?"

"I landed the balloon, Gribs!" said Fintan proudly, "All by myself!"

The torn remains of the blue and gold balloon were hanging limply from the tree where it had recently crashed. The basket had tipped sideways and was swaying in the slight breeze.

"I'm not entirely sure where we are but I've seen zebras and wildebeest and stuff so I'm pretty confident we're still in Africa. No sign of the pilot and the recovery vehicle yet though. I reckon they must've got lost."

Gribley rubbed his aching eyes and forehead, "And where is Miss Felicity, sir? Is she all right?"

"Oh yeah, she's fine," said Fintan casually, "She's having a little lie down in there."

"I am *not* fine!" snapped Felicity from the bottom of the balloon basket, "In fact, I am the exact *opposite* of fine!"

Fintan looked puzzled. He didn't know what the opposite of fine was.

"I am hot, tired, uncomfortable, thirsty, hungry and frightened!" continued Felicity, "And I am also absolutely furious! Thanks to my idiot little brother I'm stuck out here in this nasty, bug-infested nightmare of a place."

Gribley did his best to calm her down and said reassuring things about being rescued but it made no difference. Felicity wasn't going to cheer up until she was back at the hotel again, sitting by the swimming pool and reading a magazine.

"No one is coming to rescue us, Gribley!" she shrieked, "How could they? They have no idea where we are! Even *we* have no idea where we are!"

"Please try to stay calm, Miss Felicity," continued Gribley, "I'm sure the recovery vehicle will be here shortly. They merely have to follow the direction the wind is blowing. So long as we remain with the balloon they should have no trouble in locating us."

"That's true," agreed Fintan, nodding his head knowledgeably.

He had read about situations like this in *Young Adventurer* magazine. You should always stay with your vehicle so that you can be found more easily. It was a shame, though as he really wanted to get out of the tree and start exploring.

"Where d'you think we are, Gribs?" he asked, gazing around at the enormous empty space which stretched into the hazy distance in all directions.

Gribley pondered the question. The landscape was a bit different here. The earth was red and sandy, the vegetation was even sparser and a herd of long horned antelope were grazing nearby. He checked his watch and calculated the wind direction.

"It is possible that we are no longer in South Africa, sir, but have drifted into the Kalahari Desert. Perhaps somewhere beyond the Nogo Hills."

This news got Fintan very excited.

"The Nogo Hills? Brilliant!" he said, beaming broadly, "That's the place where King Zunu and his tribe were swallowed by the monster!"

Gribley wasn't sure why this should be considered 'brilliant' at all. It sounded horribly dangerous!

"And you know what that means, don't you?" continued Fintan, "I bet his diamond-studded mask is lying around here somewhere. We should go and look for it."

"An enticing possibility, sir," said Gribley, "but I'm afraid we won't be going in search of anything. We really must stay where we are."

TWENTY TWO

"I think I broke my arm, Ma!" called Suni from the middle of a large prickly bush, "It's pointing the wrong way!"

His mother didn't reply.

Suni crawled awkwardly out of the bush and looked around. He was standing at the bottom of a deep, rocky gully which had probably once been a river bed. It was now a desolate, sun-baked hole in the ground, littered with the bleached bones of wild animals.

The recovery-vehicle lay on its roof a few metres away, battered and smoking. It had bounced and rolled over so many times that it looked like a crushed sardine tin painted with zebra stripes. His mother was dangling upside-down in the driver's seat with her head stuck through the steering wheel.

"Ma?" called Suni again, "Are you OK?"

He limped back to the car with his right arm dangling by his side and his left arm sticking out sideways.

"Wake up, Ma," he said, shaking her roughly by the shoulder, "I hurt my arm, look."

Mrs Bongo opened one bloodshot eye and scowled at him.

"Who are you?" she said.

The bang on the head had caused some serious memory loss.

"It's me. Your son," explained Suni over and over again as he struggled to untangle her from the wreckage.

It wasn't easy. Mrs Bongo, who couldn't understand why this strange boy was pulling her about, wasn't cooperating. Her memory, as well as most of her teeth, had completely gone. She screamed, yelled, swore, kicked and thumped. Suni screamed, too. Especially when she bit his broken arm.

It took nearly half an hour to free her but eventually Mrs Bongo was able to stand, swaying and blinking in the sunlight. She stared at the weird-looking, shabbily dressed youth. He was battered, bruised and had bits of tree sticking out of his hair and she still didn't recognise him.

"You OK now, Ma?" he said hopefully, "It's me... your son, Suni."

"Are you?" she said, not sounding very impressed.

This was going to be a big problem. Suni relied on his mother to tell him what to do. Without her making decisions for him he had no idea what they should do next.

TWENTY THREE

Four hours passed and the large red sun continued to dip towards the horizon. There was still no sign of the recovery-vehicle.

"I *told* you they weren't coming!" ranted Felicity, still sulking in the balloon basket, "We're all going to die! We're going to be eaten alive by tigers or elephants or... or camels or something! And it's all my stupid, little brother's fault."

Fintan wanted to tell her that there weren't any tigers in Africa but decided it was probably safer to keep quiet.

"Unless we die of starvation first!" she added bitterly.

"Ah, but don't forget I brought my emergency survival kit!" said Fintan proudly, "Not such a daft idea after all, was it, eh?"

Felicity and Gribley watched eagerly as Fintan proudly opened his canvas bag. The contents, however, were a little disappointing.

Beneath the slightly bent tranquilliser darts there was a street map of Edinburgh, some raw sausages, a ball of string and a packet of very melted chocolate biscuits. The only useful items were a box of matches, a compass and a small bottle of water.

"I fear this won't last us very long, sir," said Gribley, examining the dented little plastic bottle. It was already as warm as bath water.

"There's barely enough water for one person here. We must be extremely careful if we're to avoid dehydration."

"Good point, Gribs, but already taken care of!" declared Fintan proudly.

He reached into the Luxafari picnic hamper, pulled out an enormous bottle of champagne and smiled broadly.

"I can have the water and you and Felicity can drink this!"

Gribley raised his eyebrows. Dehydration wasn't going to be a problem anymore. Getting blind drunk might be though.

The Luxafari picnic hamper was full of other fancy things, too. There were tiny triangular cucumber sandwiches, a jar of finest caviar, half a dozen smoked oysters and some weird-looking fishy pastry things that Gribley explained were called vol-au-vents. None of it was going to last very long in the heat so they decided to eat it all straight away. It would give them some much needed strength. It would probably give them hideous wind too but they couldn't afford to be fussy.

"We must be careful to ration our fluid intake, Miss Felicity," said Gribley, washing down the last oyster with a small sip of champagne.

He had been watching Felicity chugging it down in huge thirsty gulps. If she continued like that it would all be gone before sunset and Felicity would have a terrible headache in the morning.

Fintan sat on his branch and scraped out the jar of caviar with his finger. He thought it tasted like salty frogspawn but it was the only food they had.

"It's a shame we can't cook these sausages," he said, wondering whether he could use Felicity's hair drier somehow, "Maybe we could poke sticks through them and make a little fire? But what with, I wonder?"

Unfortunately neither Gribley nor Felicity were listening so neither of them noticed the early signs of Fintan having a dangerous idea. It was only when Gribley heard the sound of a match striking that he realised what was happening. Fintan had unscrewed the top from the balloon's gas bottle and had stuck a lit match inside to see if there was any gas left.

"Master Fintan, sir!" he blurted, "That's not a good idea! Please don't—"

But it was too late. The gas bottle made a deafening bang, erupted in flame and took off like a rocket, dragging what was left of the balloon with it. Felicity was hurled out of the basket and tumbled to the ground, breaking every branch on the way down.

"Sorry," said Fintan, "I didn't know it would do that. I thought it would—"

"Indeed, sir," interrupted Gribley, "Though I suggest we discuss the wisdom of your actions a little later once we have climbed down from the tree as it appears to be on fire."

TWENTY FOUR

"What did you bring me here for?" said Mrs Bongo staring around at the sun baked desolation around her. She was sitting next to the rib cage of something very large and very dead. "This isn't our house… is it?"

"I didn't bring you here, Ma," explained Suni, "We came here chasing the boy, remember? The boy who took our diamonds."

Mrs Bongo suddenly looked very interested, "Diamonds?" she said, "What diamonds? We have diamonds? I don't remember that!"

Suni nodded his head enthusiastically but it hurt so he stopped.

"Yeah. We stole them from the old lady at the hotel. But then the boy stole them from us. He swallowed them."

"Swallowed them?" repeated Mrs Bongo looking bewildered, "What did he do that for?"

Suni shrugged his shoulders but that hurt too.

"Dunno, Ma," he said, "Maybe he's a bit mad?"

Mrs Bongo rubbed her aching head and poked at her sore gums with a dirty finger, "Well, never mind that," she said, "We need to find him and get our diamonds back!"

She may have lost her memory but she hadn't forgotten how much she liked stealing things.

"Where's the boy now?"

Suni didn't know. He couldn't remember which way the balloon had been heading when they lost sight of it and there was very little wind blowing so that didn't give them any clues. He was just about to shrug his shoulders again when he heard a massive bang echo across the open country. Flocks of birds were startled into the air for miles around. They both looked up over the ridge of the gully and saw what looked like a flaming comet shoot up into the sky. Trailing behind it was a tattered blue balloon and a burning basket.

Suni smiled excitedly and pointed.

"I think he's over there, Ma."

TWENTY FIVE

"This is the worst thing that has ever happened to me!" raged Felicity, hugging herself with her bruised arms and picking bits of vol-au-vent out of her hair.

"I said I was sorry!" explained Fintan for the fifteenth time.

He couldn't understand why his sister was so upset. It had only been a short fall, after all, and she hadn't caught fire or anything! It was almost as if she'd never been thrown out of a burning tree by an exploding gas canister before!

"Get me home, Gribley! I don't like it here!" ranted Felicity, almost shaking with fury, "I need to be somewhere civilised right now! Somewhere with proper hotel rooms and comfy beds and electricity and—"

"I will certainly endeavour to do so, Miss," said Gribley trying to sound calm and optimistic.

"And me," added Fintan, "Don't forget I've got loads of experience of wilderness trekking!"

"Oh shut up, you little twerp!" snapped Felicity, "It's your silly fault we're stuck out here in the first place!"

Gribley did his best to calm everyone down and to come up with a new plan. They were, after all, stranded in the middle of a vast wilderness populated by dangerous wild animals with very little water, no food and no map. To make matters worse he was accompanied by the most accident-prone boy in the world and a girl wearing high heels and carrying a bag full of hair-care products.

Staying in the tree and waiting to be rescued was no longer an option. The balloon had gone and so had the tree. It was now just a pile of smouldering grey ash littered with a few empty caviar tins. They weren't quite sure what had happened to the balloon but it was probably several miles away and just as burnt.

"I believe our best course of action is to begin walking," announced Gribley, "According to my calculations, we should head in a south easterly direction. If all goes well we should reach civilisation within a day or two."

"Walking?" shrieked Felicity, horrified at the suggestion, "Do you realise how much these shoes cost?"

"I'm afraid it's the only option, Miss Felicity," said Gribley as patiently as he could.

Felicity was furious. She had been promised a nice, luxury balloon safari with a handsome pilot and expensive snacks. She had been promised there would be no contact with any dirt, dust, dung or wildlife and that she would be back at the hotel in time for dinner. No one had said anything about falling out of trees, sleeping in the wild or walking across the African plains!

She glared at Fintan with a look so hostile that he took a step backwards in fright. She looked as if she was about to explode like the gas bottle.

"Just you wait 'til we get back to the hotel, little brother!" she snarled, "Just you wait 'til father hears about this!"

Pausing only to snatch up the champagne bottle, she stormed off towards the rapidly setting sun.

Gribley was almost too afraid to tell her she was going the wrong way.

TWENTY SIX

Mrs Bongo and Suni spent an hour shuffling painfully across the scrubby wasteland. The sun was dipping quickly towards the horizon and the sky had turned an odd grey-pink colour but in the distance they could still see a thin plume of smoke snaking up into the sky.

"How many diamonds are there?" asked Mrs Bongo, "How big are they?"

Suni thought hard. He wasn't very good at thinking hard. It hurt his brain.

"Er... about twenty I think, Ma. And they're only little. Like peas."

Mrs Bongo smiled greedily. Twenty pea-sized diamonds would be worth a lot of money.

"And the boy has eaten them, you say? How are we going to get them back?"

"Well, you said you were going to cut them out of him, Ma. With your meat cleaver."

He pointed to the large shiny knife his mother was holding in her hand. She looked really surprised to see it there.

"You were pretending to be a cook at the hotel, Ma, remember?"

She didn't remember. But somehow it felt completely natural to be holding the dangerously sharp kitchen implement. So natural she hadn't even noticed she was carrying it. She swung it around a bit in the air and grinned a toothless grin.

By the time they reached the smoking remains of the tree it was almost dark. Mrs Bongo stopped, put a finger to her lips and made a shh noise. Ahead of them in the gloom they could just about make out some blurry shapes moving about. There was something lying on the ground, probably trying to get to sleep. In fact there were three somethings.

"Was the boy alone?" whispered Mrs Bongo into her son's ear.

Suni shook his head again and winced in pain. He'd forgotten it hurt to do that.

"No," he hissed, "I think there were two other people with him. A teenage girl and an old man. So…"

He paused to do a little mental arithmetic, "So there were three of them."

His mother was delighted to hear this. A boy, a teenage girl and an old man. It was going to be really easy!

"Excellent," she said, raising her meat cleaver and creeping forwards, "Come on, er... what's your name? Son. Let's get our diamonds back!"

Suddenly one of the somethings jerked its head up and roared a terrifying, bloodcurdling roar. Mrs Bongo and Suni froze in fright. They were creeping up on three massive, hairy lions which were happily chomping away on Fintan's raw sausages.

"Run!" said Mrs Bongo.

Suni, who was glad his mother was making decisions again, turned around and ran as fast as he could. The lions abandoned what was left of the sausages and bounded hungrily after them.

"Over there, quick," yelled Mrs Bongo, "Get up that tree!"

It was the only other tree for miles around and they knew they had to get to it before the lions caught up with them. It's an interesting fact but there's something about being chased by lions that can make you forget all about broken arms, concussion and dislocated shoulders. It's the sort of thing that can inspire you to run faster than you ever thought possible and to climb the most difficult of trees like a huge, terrified squirrel. Within seconds, both Suni and his mum were ten feet off the ground and clinging tightly to the tree's chunky branches. The lions stopped at the foot of the tree looking angry, disappointed and very hungry. They growled menacingly and began circling around the trunk. They knew the humans would have to climb down eventually and they were prepared to wait.

It took a few minutes for Mrs Bongo and Suni to realise they had made it to safety and for their breathing to slow down and their hearts to stop pounding. That was when they realised they were in a thorn tree. All its branches were covered in long spiky thorns. They probably weren't going to get much sleep.

TWENTY SEVEN

"I'm tired," moaned Felicity, from somewhere behind the others, "My feet hurt and I don't feel very well."

They had been walking all night to avoid the sweltering heat of the day but had only covered a few miles. It hadn't been easy. The ground was soft and sandy with patches of coarse, spiky grass. Felicity had fallen over several times and lost her favourite sparkly shoes in the darkness. This had made it a bit easier to walk but had put her in an even worse mood. She had also lost her enormous bag full of evening dresses and hairdryers which she had decided was her 'stupid brother's fault'.

Gribley and Fintan stopped walking and looked back. It wasn't quite dawn but in the dim light they could see the poor girl's face was a sweaty mess, streaked with black eye make-up and smeared with lipstick.

"And I want to go home!"

She wobbled about a bit then burped, fell to her knees and dropped the empty champagne bottle on the sandy ground.

"Oh dear," said Gribley.

"Is she drunk?" asked Fintan as his older sister toppled over sideways and lay in an awkward heap.

"I'm afraid so, sir," said Gribley, "I did caution Miss Felicity not to drink too much of the champagne but unfortunately she has consumed the whole bottle."

This explained a lot. Fintan finally understood why she had been in such an annoyingly good mood for the last few hours. She had even been singing really badly while they walked. Gribley and Fintan had been forced to listen to three hours of her tunelessly belting out her favourite pop songs, as well putting up with a lot of silly giggling.

"She also appears to be suffering from exhaustion, sir."

Fintan rolled his eyes and tutted, "Typical!" he said, "No stamina at all! Can't even walk across the Kalahari Desert without getting tired!"

Gribley knelt down beside the sweaty girl and tried to persuade her to keep moving.

"If you can just manage to walk a little further, Miss, we can rest in the shade."

He gestured to a small clump of spindly trees about half a mile ahead. Dawn was breaking and the air was already beginning to warm up.

"I'm not going any further, Grill-bee!" she slurred, "I want my nice comfy bed and I want it now! Also I want my breakfast... toast please with marla... with marla-made."

"She's gone nuts, Gribs!" observed Fintan, "Lost the plot!"

"Come along now, Miss Felicity," continued Gribley trying very hard to sound encouraging, "You can't sleep out here in the open. We really need to get somewhere shady first."

"Oh, and I also want my shoes," she said pointing vaguely at her dirty, blistered feet, "Where are my shoes? They were my favourite ones, you know. Sparkly and shiny like stars!"

"Indeed, Miss, but we——"

"Just like stars they were! All lovely and sharkly and spiny!"

"Just a little further," pleaded Gribley.

"But guess what happened?" gibbered Felicity, "... my hobber... my horrible little brother made me lose them! In the stupid hot desert!"

"No I didn't," said Fintan sounding offended, "It's not my fault you wore them."

At the sound of her brother's voice, Felicity's temper reached boiling point. She lurched to her feet and stumbled towards him flailing her fists wildly.

"You've ruined my life!" she yelled before falling over again and planting her face in the ground.

She was completely senseless. For a moment everything was silent. Nothing was heard but the gentle stirrings of desert insects greeting the dawn. Fintan and Gribley stared at each other.

"Well, *I'm* not carrying her!" stated Fintan abruptly, planting his hands on his hips.

TWENTY EIGHT

"Can lions climb trees, Ma?" asked Suni, shifting around uncomfortably on his prickly tree branch.

"How should I know?" snapped his mother, "I didn't grow up in the bush, did I! I'm not Tarzan!"

She paused for a moment unable to remember whether this was true or not. She had no memory at all of where she had grown up.

"Don't think I did anyway. Can't remember."

Below them the three huge lions were still pacing around looking hungry but very patient. Every now and then they would let out a low, rumbling growl and stare upwards slowly licking their jaws.

Suni thought for a moment, "Well there's one thing I'm pretty sure about, because Mrs Nyala told us in school; young lions can definitely climb trees. But these lions don't look like young lions do they, Ma? They look quite big and heavy. Maybe they're too big to climb the tree?"

Mrs Bongo sighed. She'd had a terrible night. The tree had been painful, the lions had been terrifying, her head still hurt and her son had been annoying. All night! She was feeling more than a little irritable.

"After all," continued Suni, "They haven't climbed up yet, have they. And we've been up here for hours! Maybe that means they can't climb it. I mean if they could then they'd probably—"

"Oh just shut up, will you!" shrieked Mrs Bongo."

To Suni's surprise all three lions suddenly flinched and hurried a few steps away from the tree. It was as if they couldn't stand the sound of his mother's horrible, rasping voice. Most people agreed it was a particularly nasty sound; a bit like someone sawing through a steel pipe with a rusty blade, only worse.

"Ma!" hissed Suni, "Do that again!"

"Do what again?" she barked.

The lions retreated even further looking visibly distressed. They definitely hated her voice!

"Shout some more, Ma. It's frightening the lions away!"

Mrs Bongo glowered at the weird-looking boy who claimed to be her son. Was he really suggesting that the sound of her voice was so horrible that it could scare off the most fearsome carnivore in Africa? What an insulting thing to say! Feeling hugely annoyed, she launched into a really loud, nasty, foul-mouthed barrage of angry words. The lions whimpered as if they were being stung on the eardrums by bees then fled as fast as they could.

"Thanks, Ma," said Suni, climbing down the tree.

TWENTY NINE

Back at Hotel Impala, Inspector Kudu was worried. His prime suspect, Fintan Fedora, had gone missing. According to the boy's anxious parents Fintan had left the previous morning for a balloon safari and failed to return. His sister and the family butler were also missing. What on earth was the boy up to? Was he on the run? Had he taken the others as hostages? Fintan was looking guiltier than ever. There was no point hanging around at the hotel any longer. It was time for him to head out and apprehend the young diamond thief!

The inspector was just getting into his car when two ragged looking men wobbled up on even more ragged looking bicycles. They didn't appear to know how to ride them very well. One of the men, who had two black eyes and a broken nose, rode straight into a parked car and fell off over the handlebars.

"Excuse me... hello?" said the other man, dumping his bike on the concrete, and staggering forwards holding his badly bruised face, "Are you the police?"

The inspector found it hard to understand anything the man was saying. Partly because he was out of breath from cycling for miles through the bush, but mostly because he had a broken jaw which flapped like a loose shoe-sole when he spoke.

"Yes, I am the police," confirmed the inspector, "I am Inspector Kudubenikubiza of the South African police. How can I help you?"

"I want to report a theft," mumbled the man, "Somebody stole my balloon!"

There was a short, disbelieving pause.

"Somebody stole your what?" asked Inspector Kudu.

"My balloon!" repeated the handsome pilot, who wasn't quite so handsome anymore because of the broken jaw and various other cuts and bruises.

"Your balloon?" said the inspector, thinking he meant the sort of balloon you blew up for birthday parties. It wasn't much of a crime! Certainly not the sort of thing that you bothered the South African police with.

"Yes!" insisted the pilot, "My hot air balloon!"

Suddenly the inspector understood what he meant.

"Ah, I see!" he said, sounding much more interested, "And did your hot air balloon belong to the 'Luxafari' company by any chance?"

Both men nodded. Even the recovery vehicle driver understood the word 'Luxafari'. The inspector's mind was made up.

"This way, please," he said, escorting the two men into the hotel lobby and taking out his official notebook, "Tell me everything that happened!"

The pilot sat on one of the expensive white sofas and tried to explain it all, pausing every now and then to push his bottom jaw back into position. Inspector Kudu nodded and took page after page of notes. Admittedly, he didn't quite understand everything that was being said. Hardly any of it actually. There was something about cleavers and anchors and bicycles but it was all a bit vague. He nodded a lot, kept writing and hoped he wasn't missing anything important. But in his mind everything was very clear. This was obviously the work of that notorious diamond thief, Fintan Fedora! The cunning little devil must have beaten up the pilot and the driver and escaped by hijacking the Luxafari hot air balloon!

THIRTY

"Nearly there," announced Fintan happily, as they approached the clump of shady thorn trees.

Gribley nodded breathlessly, but was too tired to reply. He had been carrying an apparently lifeless Felicity on his back for about 20 minutes, though it had seemed like an eternity. Every now and then she would jerk about, belch and mumble something about killing her brother, but mostly she was dead to the world.

"Hey look, Gribs," said Fintan, "There are people under the trees!"

It was true. Ahead of them, sitting quietly in the shade, were two Africans watching their approach. They looked a little surprised to see strangers wandering around in their neighbourhood, but seemed completely relaxed about it. Both of them stood up and strolled casually over. The man was stick-thin and almost completely naked apart from a ragged loin cloth while the woman had a tiny sleeping baby strapped across her front. Both were carrying sharp spears and bows.

"This is really brilliant!" whispered Fintan, "Proper African tribes people!"

The Africans smiled very broad, friendly smiles and began speaking in the strangest language Fintan had ever heard. It sounded like a stream of humming and clicking sounds and made no sense whatsoever.

"Hello," said Fintan excitedly, "Nice to meet you!"

The Africans continued smiling until they noticed the sad state of the unconscious girl. After a sudden hurried exchange of bizarre clicking speech the man gently lifted her from Gribley's exhausted back and carried her into the shade. Fintan watched in fascination as the woman set about digging into the sand with her spear and unearthed something that looked like a dirty brown cucumber.

"What's she doing, Gribs?" he asked.

"I believe she is finding water for your sister, sir," said Gribley, wiping the sweat from his brow.

Fintan was confused, "Water? In some dirty old cucumber?" he said.

"It is a sort of root, sir. There should be a small amount of water stored inside."

As they spoke, the woman broke the root in half and scraped out a handful of white squashy pulp. She shaped it into a ball, held it over Felicity's gaping mouth and squeezed it until a stream of water dripped out.

"Wow!" said Fintan, "These people are brilliant! Are they Zulus or what, Gribs?"

Gribley shook his head, "No, sir. Judging by their appearance and their distinctive clicking language, I'd say they are of a group called the San people."

Fintan nodded as if he knew all about them, "Oh right," he said, "And that's because of all the sand round here, I suppose? There's not a lot else to name a tribe after is there."

"Not sand, sir. The *San* people."

Fintan looked blank.

"It's the general name for many individual tribal groups in this part of Africa, such as the Naro and the Kua and the Kung... or you might call them the famous bushmen of the Kalahari."

"Bushmen?" said Fintan excitedly, "Oh wow! I've definitely heard of them! There was a thing in *Young Adventurer* magazine about them once. They're brilliant! They still live a lot like their ancestors did hundreds of years ago and can run for hours and hours in the heat chasing wild animals and stuff."

Gribley nodded, "That is quite correct, sir. They are a very impressive people."

Gribley sat beneath the trees next to where a fully rehydrated Felicity was now snoring contentedly.

"Gangans." he said, smiling at the two Africans.

"Il korel har!" replied the man, stunned that this strange foreigner knew how to say 'thank you' in his language.

Fintan was stunned, too. The amount of amazing things his butler could do never ceased to astonish him.

"Blimey, Gribs!" he breathed, joining the others beneath the trees away from the growing heat of the morning, "I didn't know you spoke Zulu!"

"It's not Zulu, sir, it's Nama. One of the many Bushman languages. Though I'm afraid I've become a little rusty over the years. However, as luck would have it, I thought to bring along my Bushman phrase-book."

He produced a small volume from his top pocket.

"You're a genius, Gribs!" smiled Fintan who had only brought his Chinese phrase-book and a beginner's guide to the butterflies of Canada.

The smiling woman passed Fintan a scooped-out handful of the damp root.

"Gang nam!" he said, which wasn't bad for a first attempt.

While Felicity slept Fintan and Gribley watched in amazement as the African man produced a bow and arrow and shot a squirrel out of a tree with pinpoint accuracy. The woman speared a small brown bird, dug up more roots and built a fire. It appeared they had been invited to stay for breakfast.

THIRTY ONE

"This is the place. Stop here," said the formerly handsome pilot pointing out of the police car window.

"Pardon?" asked Inspector Kudu, "Did you say stop here?"

The pilot nodded. It was still difficult to understand anything the poor man said. The bandage tied tightly around his head, which was holding his bottom jaw on, didn't help. Kudu stopped the car and climbed out looking very serious. He was on the hunt for clues.

They were at the site of the Luxafari balloon theft. Mr and Mrs Fedora, who had insisted on coming with them, got out of the back seat and followed along close behind him. Flavian stayed in the car, wide-eyed and trembling.

"Be careful not to touch anything!" warned the inspector, "Remember, this is a crime scene."

Mr Fedora nodded while Mrs Fedora held on to his arm looking very worried, "Oh I do hope they're all right!" she said, choking back the tears, "My poor children! All alone out there in the unknown!"

"They'll be fine, I'm sure," said her husband, patting her supportively on her shoulder, "Gribley knows what he's doing… and as for our Fintan! Well, he might be a bit troublesome at times, but we both know he can survive anything! The boy's virtually indestructible! It's *Africa* I'm worried about!"

"But what about Felicity?" sobbed Mrs Fedora taking out a large hankie and blowing her nose, "The poor girl's so delicate! She's never been anywhere without room-service and air-conditioning before! How's she going to cope with all that… all that… wilderness?"

She gestured weakly towards the enormous African emptiness in front of them. It was a terrifying thought. Mr Fedora shook his head. He couldn't think of anything reassuring to say.

"Be strong, dearest, be strong!" he mumbled, wiping a tear from the corner of his eye.

Inspector Kudu produced a map from his pocket and checked it against a printed report of the previous day's weather.

"North-easterly," he mumbled to himself, gazing off into the distance.

He turned his attention to the ground and examined the flattened grass where the fighting had taken place.

"Hmm… interesting." he mused.

"What is?" enquired Mr Fedora, "What's interesting?"

The inspector pointed to various dents and scuff marks on the ground which, to the untrained eye, just looked like various dents and scuff marks.

"Too many footprints," he declared, "I'd say there were, let's see… seven people here, not five."

"I already told you that!" said the pilot looking surprised.

The inspector nodded in agreement, without understanding a single word.

"Good," he said.

He followed a vague disturbance in the dusty soil to the place where the recovery-vehicle had been parked.

"Tyre tracks," he announced to himself, nodding knowledgeably, number 35 rough-terrain radials if I'm not mistaken" "Just as I thought! Someone stole the truck, too!"

The pilot looked surprised, "But… I already told you that, too! Back at the hotel when you were taking notes!" he said, clutching his wobbly jaw, "Weren't you listening?"

Kudu looked blankly at the pilot then glanced at his watch, "Er... quarter to eleven," he said. "Right, everyone back in the car. We have a trail to follow!"

THIRTY TWO

Mrs Bongo and Suni were also following a trail. They had found three sets of footprints leading away from the burnt tree and were tracking them across the sand. One of the tracks had apparently been made by someone wearing high-heeled shoes who, for some reason, had veered wildly from side to side. They had fallen over quite a lot, too, judging by the occasional girl-shaped dents in the ground.

"Look, Ma," announced Suni, pointing ahead excitedly, "Something shiny!"

Mrs Bongo knelt down and examined what her son had found.

"Interesting," she said.

It was a very sparkly pair of women's shoes with high stiletto heels. Not the sort of thing you usually found in the middle of the Kalahari Desert.

"Do you think they're the boy's shoes, Ma?" said Suni, "The boy who ate our diamonds?"

"Hmm?" mused Mrs Bongo, who was too busy wondering whether the fancy shoes would fit her, "What? Well, how should I know? I can't remember anything since that bang on the head, *can* I!"

Suni's face dropped. He had forgotten he was the one in charge now, "Oh yeah." he mumbled sadly, "Well… they don't really look much like boy's shoes, do they. Maybe they're the girl's shoes then? There was a girl in the balloon, too, I think. Was there a girl, Ma?"

"Size five," said his mother cramming one of the sparkly shoes onto her filthy, old foot, "Just right!"

Encouraged that they were probably on the right trail, they continued to follow it for another few hours. Every now and then Mrs Bongo paused to pick up more surprising treasures. She acquired several posh dresses which didn't fit but were much nicer than the one she was wearing, a hairdryer and an assortment of brushes, lotions and cosmetics as well as a very smart bag to carry them all in.

The only thing Suni found was a small pile of abandoned tranquilliser darts which he trod on, then went cross-eyed and passed out.

THIRTY THREE

After an interesting breakfast of charred tree roots, singed songbird and roast squirrel, Fintan and Gribley slept contentedly in the shade of the trees. Felicity was the first to wake up. She opened one dirt-encrusted eye and stared blearily around attempting to focus. Then she screamed.

"Don't kill me!" she shrieked, "Don't eat me!"

She had never seen Bushmen before, not even on the TV as they rarely appeared on the shopping channel.

Gribley sat up abruptly and tried to calm her down, "There's no cause for alarm, Miss Felicity," he said, "These people are quite harmless. In fact they have been very kind to us."

Felicity still didn't like the look of them and shuffled backwards against a tree trunk. In her eyes they were nothing but wild people; savage, uncivilised and dangerous! They had no clothes! Which meant they had obviously never heard of fashion! They probably couldn't even name a single designer label!

"I don't trust them, Gribley," she muttered, her eyes darting about in terror, "Are you sure they're not cannibals?"

"Quite sure, Miss," said Gribley reassuringly, "They just cooked us a lovely meal. There is still a little left if you are hungry?"

Right on cue the San woman came over and offered Felicity the remains of the roast squirrel. She took one look at it, screamed again, then scrambled further under the trees and threw up very loudly.

Fintan raised his head from what had been a really good sleep and yawned contentedly, "Afternoon, everyone," he said.

He was feeling happier and more relaxed than he had felt in a long time. His money worries had been put to the back of his mind and almost forgotten about. This was exactly the sort of African experience he'd been hoping for: sleeping in the open, meeting exotic local people, eating exotic local food. This was the *real* Africa! It was perfect. Well, perfect apart from the girl in the expensive dress who was crouched under the trees and making revolting vomiting noises.

He spent the afternoon trying to learn a few of the San people's skills. Luckily the San were very patient teachers. His attempts at arrow-making weren't bad but his arrows turned out to be too bent to fly in a straight line. The only thing he shot was Gribley's phrase-book; luckily it wasn't in Gribley's pocket at the time. Animal tracking was quite tricky, too. No matter how many times he was shown the tiny, very subtle signs that wild creatures had left behind, he could see nothing at all. Well, apart from the huge pile of rhino dung, which he trod in anyway. He even tried learning a few words of the Bushman's language but it was far too difficult. He sounded like a cross between a leaky tap and goose having a coughing fit.

As evening approached, Gribley pointed towards the distant Nogo Hills and asked the San people if it was the way back to the city. He used a stick to draw the rough shape of a tall building in the sand. Both of the San looked concerned and spoke in a fast, agitated way. They appeared to agree that it was the right direction, but didn't think it was a good idea. Instead, they pointed to the South and gestured that he should go around the hills. Gribley was confused. Going round the hills would add hundreds of miles to their journey.

"What are they saying, Gribs?" asked Fintan.

Gribley pulled the bent arrow out of his phrasebook and looked up the word they were repeating over and over. It was 'danger'.

"They are telling us we should avoid the Nogo Hills, sir. Apparently it is a dangerous place."

Fintan was overjoyed, "I *knew* it!" he said triumphantly, "I knew the legend was true! I bet they're talking about the Nogo Hills monster. The one that swallows people whole! Can you ask them if it's all true please, Gribs? Go on, ask them about the invisible monster and King Zunu and his diamond-studded mask!"

"I shall try, sir," sighed Gribley, "Though I fear my phrasebook is intended more for basic conversation. I doubt it includes phrases such as 'diamond-studded mask' and 'invisible monster'."

It was a long and difficult process, but, with the help of the phrasebook, several drawings in the sand and a lot of pointing, Gribley finally got an answer. Somewhere in the Nogo Hills lived an invisible monster that swallowed people whole! Two hundred years earlier it had swallowed King Zunu along with fifty of his finest, bravest warriors; all in one gulp! The greedy king had gone there looking for more and more diamonds until the monster put a stop to it. And it was still there guarding the hills.

"I told you didn't I, Gribs!" said a very excited Fintan, "It's all true! And that means King Zunu's diamond-studded mask is still up there somewhere!"

"Oh please!" sneered Felicity, who had stopped being sick and returned to being miserable, "What a load of old nonsense!"

"No, it isn't!" asserted Fintan, "You don't know what you're talking about!"

Felicity tutted and rolled her eyes, "It's just a silly superstitious story, that's all. The sort of silly story that only stupid, primitive people believe. I mean, come on! These people haven't even invented clothes yet! Or prams!"

She gestured rudely towards the woman with her baby in a rough sling, "They obviously don't know anything at all!"

Fintan felt his blood pressure rising. There was going to be a fight. It had been brewing for several days and there was no stopping it.

"Oh yes they do!" he snapped, "They know a lot more than *you* do, that's for sure!"

"Ha!" retorted his sister, "Ask them which sort of shampoo is best for dry hair then. Go on, ask them! They look like they've never used a volumising conditioner in their lives! Unless it was mud!"

"Yeah, but that's not important, is it!" argued Fintan, "They know about the important stuff."

Felicity stood as close to her brother as she could and poked him in the chest with a finger, "Huh, well obviously you'd think that, wouldn't you, you scruffy little weasel!"

Gribley decided he'd better intervene before anyone got punched, and dragged the two of them apart. As the yelling continued the Bushman couple backed away slightly and exchanged a surprised look, "What's wrong with these people?" whispered the woman, placing her hands over her baby's ears.

Her husband shook his head sadly, "I don't understand them," he said, "They're not very civilised are they!"

THIRTY FOUR

It took Mrs Bongo at least half an hour to realise her son had been tranquillised again, and that he wasn't just being lazy. She had wasted a lot of time and energy shouting at him to get up and had become really angry when he ignored her. She had tried kicking him, calling him insulting names and threatening him with all sorts of unpleasant punishments, but he had hadn't budged an inch. She had even dragged him along by his ankle for a while but it had been much too exhausting. After that she had given up and just sat around on the hot sand, mumbling to herself.

It was really annoying not being able to remember anything from before the car crash. All her memories had just vanished. The insensible lump of a youth had told her they were trying to get their diamonds back but she had no memory of possessing them in the first place or of the English boy who had stolen them. It was all very frustrating. The unconscious lump was also apparently her son but she had no memory of him either!

For a while, she had thought about going off on her own and leaving him behind for the vultures to snack on, but had changed her mind. It didn't seem like a very motherly thing to do. In the end she just sat there and waited until he woke up.

Eventually Suni opened one dirt-encrusted eye and gazed groggily around.

"What happened, Ma?" he mumbled.

He had been lying in the afternoon sun for five hours and felt terrible. His face was plastered with sweat and snot and coated with sand and flies. His mother was sitting miserably nearby.

"You trod on these things," she said, holding up a tranquilliser dart which she had pulled from the sole of his shoe.

There had been about a dozen of them there earlier, poking right through into his foot like a foul-smelling hedgehog.

"You've been out of it for ages."

Suni stared blearily at the tranquilliser darts and the holes in his worn-out old trainer.

"Trod on them?" he said, finding it hard to believe, "What… they were just lying around on the ground? In the middle of the desert?"

His mother nodded, "Some idiot must have dropped them there," she said.

Suni sat up and rubbed the muck from his face. He noticed the trail of footprints they had been following across the sand and felt a new wave of anger flood through his soggy brain. He knew exactly who that idiot was.

It was that horrible interfering English boy again!

Mrs Bongo hauled herself to her aching feet and stretched, making a loud groaning noise.

"Come on, get up now," she demanded, "We've wasted far too much time already and I want my diamonds back!"

She grabbed her son by the wrist and yanked him upright. There was a nasty bone-wrenching sound. Suni screamed with pain, blacked out and collapsed again. She had forgotten his arm was broken.

THIRTY FIVE

Fintan, Gribley and Felicity had said goodbye to the Bushmen, thanked them for their help and were continuing on their journey. Well, Fintan and Gribley had anyway: Felicity had just stomped off, still in a sulky mood and still in a hurry to get back to the hotel. Despite the Bushmen's warning, they had chosen to take the most direct route home and were beginning their slow ascent of the Nogo Hills. Gribley was leading the way, followed by a very excited Fintan who couldn't stop thinking about what might lay ahead of them. Felicity trudged along several metres behind, moaning about everything she could think of.

"I will never forgive you for making me lose my favourite shoes," she muttered at Fintan's back, "My feet *really* hurt!"

Fintan ignored her. He was bored of arguing about it, and anyway, his head was full of thoughts about King

Zunu's diamond-studded mask! They were walking in the footsteps of those ancient, lost warriors. Heading into the legendary Nogo Hills, home of the invisible monster that swallowed people whole! He knew the bit about the monster was just a story of course. It was one of those old tribal myths. But it was a *brilliant* myth! The bit about the diamond mask, however, was probably true! And he had every intention of finding it. After all, he was really good at stuff like that. He had already discovered the mythical Chocoplum fruit, deep in the Brazilian rainforest. And he had also found the Golden Moon dragon in the ruins of a lost Chinese village. He knew it was only a matter of time before he would be holding King Zunu's mask in his hands.

Behind them, the evening sun sank below the horizon and the Nogo Hills turned an eerie shade of blue. Prickly shrubs and scattered rocks began to look more sinister, like weird twisted creatures lurking in the gloom. Despite her sore feet, Felicity hurried to catch up with Gribley. She was feeling a little unsafe. Somewhere up ahead strange animal noises echoed through the growing darkness. Something was making the most unearthly noise. It was a weird high pitched whooping sound like a gale of demonic laughter. And it was coming closer.

"What is it, Gribley?" hissed Felicity, staring around in terror, "I don't like it. Make it go away. Kill it, Gribley, kill it!"

"There's no need to be alarmed, Miss Felicity," said Gribley in his most reassuring tone, "I believe we are hearing the sound of hyenas; a species which primarily scavenges for food. They are unlikely to attack us."

Felicity wasn't reassured, "What do you mean, 'unlikely'?" she said, "*How* unlikely? Are you saying there's still a *chance* they'll attack us?"

"Just a very small chance, Miss. But only if they perceive their prey to be injured or weak and defenceless."

There was a brief pause in which Felicity's brain imagined terrible things happening to her, and her best dress.

"But...*I'm* injured!" she gasped, grabbing Gribley's arm, "Have you seen these blisters on my feet? And I've got the worst sunburn *ever*! Plus I'm really tired which means I'm weak and defenceless, too! Oh my God, I'm going to die! Help me, Gribley, what can I do?"

"Well…" mused Fintan thoughtfully, "I suppose there is *one* thing you could do. I read about it in *Young Adventurer* magazine once."

His sister was desperate. So desperate that she was even willing to listen to something her younger brother said.

"What is it? Tell me! Anything. I'll do anything! I want to live!"

"You won't like it," said Fintan.

"Tell me," demanded his sister, darkly.

Fintan scratched his chin, "Well it was quite a while ago when I read it so I don't remember it all that well."

"Try!" hissed Felicity, grabbing him by his shirt collar.

"OK, well I'm pretty sure the article said that hyenas have a brilliant sense of smell and that they hunt their prey by sniffing them out."

"And?" urged Felicity, impatient to hear the important bit.

"And it said that they don't like bad smells... like dung and stuff."

His sister nodded her head vigorously, "Don't like dung, right. But what do I *do*?"

"Right, well this is the bit I'm not too sure about but I *think* it said you need to disguise your human smell... by rolling in some dung or something. And then they'll leave you alone."

For a moment Felicity's panic stricken face went blank. Her brain found itself struggling with a terrible dilemma, and seized up. Which was worse? Covering herself in dung or being eaten by hyenas? Dung was revolting. It was poo! But on the plus side you could wash it off afterwards. Being eaten by hyenas, however, wasn't something you recovered from. It was sort of fatal!

"I need dung!" she insisted, "Get me some dung!"

The next few minutes were possibly the most enjoyable of Fintan's whole life. He stood and watched in joyous disbelief as his horrible sister squatted on the ground and voluntarily smothered her face, arms and legs with large stinking dollops of wildebeest dung. She was actually doing it!

"Don't forget your hair," suggested Fintan helpfully.

Gribley started to suspect something wasn't quite right. He didn't like the way Fintan was biting his lip to avoid bursting out laughing.

"Are you *quite* sure this is necessary, sir?" he enquired, "I must say I have never read anything which suggested coating oneself in dung as a protective measure."

"Necessary?" said Fintan, fighting back a giggle, "Well, I'm not sure really, Gribs. I might have got it completely wrong, but if it's making Felicity feel safer, then… that's a good thing, isn't it?"

"There," announced Felicity having just finished rubbing some incredibly stinky baboon droppings into her scalp, "I'm all done. Now how about you two?"

Gribley said nothing but stared awkwardly at his shoes. Fintan made a face to suggest he might be considering it, "Um…? No, I'm all right, thanks," he said.

THIRTY SIX

Meanwhile, Inspector Kudu was getting closer. He had followed the recovery-vehicle's tyre tracks to the bone-strewn gully where the wrecked vehicle lay, upside down and battered. After this it had just been a matter of tracking the two sets of footprints which led to the burnt tree. Everyone climbed out of the car except Flavian, of course, who still wasn't feeling any better. The inspector shone his torch beam around in search of more clues and lighted on something hanging from a charred tree.

"Look there!" said the previously handsome pilot, wincing in pain as his broken jaw clicked out of place again, "My balloon basket!"

The sad, blackened remains of the Luxafari basket swung slowly in the warm night time breeze.

"Aha!" announced Kudu proudly, "I'd say we've found our missing balloon basket! And it looks like it has been on fire."

"My luxury picnic things too," added the pilot, pointing to the mess on the ground.

Kudu examined the scattered caviar jars, which had all been licked clean and the chewed remains of a few raw sausages. They were surrounded by a mess of very large animal footprints. "Hmm," he said sombrely, "Lion. Definitely lion."

Mrs Fedora almost fainted, "Oh my goodness!" she said, clutching her husband for support, "Lions? My poor children!"

"Do not panic, Madam," continued Kudu, "The lions appear only to have eaten the Luxafari picnic food. There's no sign of anyone being hurt."

He shone his torch at the ground and noticed the footprints split into two groups.

"Let's see… five sets of human prints and three of lions. The lions appear to have chased two of the humans over there to that tree… while the other three humans headed off in that direction."

The inspector pointed off into the darkness.

"And I'd say one of them was wearing high-heeled shoes."

"High-heels?" beamed Mrs Fedora, "Did you hear that, dear? It's our Felicity! She's alive!"

THIRTY SEVEN

The hyenas were very close now. Their bizarre shrieking sounds cut through the darkness like horribly unfunny laughter. Fintan could see their yellow eyes glowing in the torchlight.

"I suggest we just keep walking and act confidently," said Gribley, "I'm sure they're just curious. We're quite safe."

Every now and then one of the hyena pack would run cautiously towards them for a closer look then turn and run away again.

"Gribs, they've got spots, look!" said Fintan as the large hairy creature disappeared back into the dark.

"Indeed, sir," agreed Gribley, "They are spotted hyenas, Latin name 'crocuta crocuta', popularly known as the 'laughing hyena'."

"Oh right!" said Fintan, "Any idea what they're laughing about?"

Gribley glanced uncertainly at Fintan. Sometimes he couldn't be sure whether the boy was joking or not.

"They're not *actually* laughing, sir," he said, "It merely sounds like they are."

"I knew that," said Fintan, nodding sagely.

Another large hyena ran right up to Felicity and bared its nasty looking fangs then turned and ran away, yelping.

"Get away, you beast!" yelled Felicity, sounding slightly insane, "You can't hurt me! I'm protected!"

Bizarrely, the girl's thick coating of animal dung really did seem to be working. Any hyenas that came within sniffing distance of Felicity looked genuinely distressed. One by one the entire pack decided they would rather be somewhere less smelly and hurriedly ran off.

"Hey look, Gribs," said a surprised Fintan, "The dung thing works!"

Gribley was just as surprised, "It would appear so, sir," he said, "Perhaps your sister inadvertently applied some lion dung."

It was entirely possible. There could easily have been lion droppings among the random assortment she had scooped up in the darkness. None of them would have known the difference. Not even Gribley's incredible range of knowledge included identifying different types of wild animal poo.

"I believe hyenas are afraid of the scent of lions which would explain their reaction."

"It would," agreed Fintan, "Either that or they just don't like Felicity."

THIRTY EIGHT

The higher they climbed, the rockier the Nogo Hills became, until gradually they flattened out into a broad, bare plateau. Only a handful of spiky trees and plants managed to grow there. The trees had spread their roots over the rocky ground like long fingers desperately clinging to the thin layer of soil. It was unnervingly quiet up there, too. Since the hyenas had run off the silence had been feeling a bit spooky.

"This is rather interesting," said Gribley as his torch's beam fell on a large outcrop of rock, "There appears to be some sort of drawing over here."

The three of them stopped and took a closer look. The whole surface of the rock was covered with the unmistakable outlines of rhinos and buffalo, all beautifully drawn in a dark shade of red. There were also strange geometric shapes, giraffes, antelope and hippos.

"How fascinating!" mused Gribley, "I've seen photographs of these paintings. They're thousands of years old! Made by the ancient San people; ancestors of the ones we met earlier."

"Really?" said Fintan, "Cool!"

"Indeed, sir. We must be in an area of great historical and magical significance; a sacred place for the San. Perhaps that was why they didn't wish us to come up here?"

"Could be," said Fintan, "Well, that and the dangerous, invisible monster, obviously."

"It's graffiti!" snapped Felicity disapprovingly, "That's what it is!"

Gribley disagreed. A short, heated discussion followed as he attempted to explain the difference between ancient, cultural artefacts and mindless graffiti. Fintan wandered off, stepping over a tangle of tree roots. He was fed up with arguments and he was also fed up with his dung-covered sister smelling like a blocked drain. He stood beneath a battered old tree, shone his torch around and spotted more rock art close to the ground. This art was a bit different. It showed a group of human figures standing in a line. The man at the front of the line had been drawn about twice the size of the others and was wearing a large, elaborate tribal mask. Little lines had been painted around the edges of the mask as if it was shining brightly; as if it was covered with diamonds. Fintan's face lit up with excitement.

"Gribs!" he shouted, "Come and look at this! I think I've found King Zunu!"

Gribley stopped arguing at once and came over to join him.

"See?" continued Fintan, pointing at the rock, "It's got the diamond-studded mask and everything! And look at this bit; the figure on the end here's got one really long leg! It goes all the way down to the ground. What do you suppose that means?"

"Curious," said Gribley, "That is most unusual."

"Huh! So that's your King Zunu is it?" snorted Felicity sarcastically, "And I suppose there's a picture of the invisible monster that swallows people whole, too?"

Fintan stared at her as if she was an idiot, "Well, of course not," he said, "It's invisible!"

He rolled his eyes and shared an exasperated look with Gribley.

Suddenly there was a strange creaking noise, the ground trembled and all three of them plummeted down into a deep, black hole. After a few terrifying seconds of falling through the darkness they hit a hard, unseen floor.

Felicity screamed again as Fintan landed on top of her amid a shower of earth, dead leaves and twigs.

"Get off me, you idiot!" she yelled, pushing him roughly aside.

Fintan clambered over what felt like a pile of dirt littered with wriggling insects.

"What just happened?" he spluttered, spitting out bits of tree bark, "Where are we?"

"I'm afraid I'm not sure, sir," said Gribley, groping around for his torch which had disappeared somewhere beneath the scattered debris.

It had been a bit of a shock. Without warning they had dropped from a dark, rocky plateau to an even darker, rockier hole in the ground. The impenetrable blackness was filled with the strong smell of decay and musty, dead leaves.

"Are we in a cave, Gribs?" asked Fintan, "It smells like a cave."

Gribley found his torch and switched it on. They were definitely in a cave.

About ten metres above them they could see a small patch of starry night sky. Other than that there was nothing but bare rock and tree roots. Then the torch died.

"I believe this is what is commonly known as a 'sinkhole'," said Gribley, "There must have been a layer of soil and plant matter covering the entrance to the hole, rather like a trap door. Presumably it accumulated there over many years then gave way under our weight."

Fintan nodded even though no one could see him in the dark, "A sink hole, eh?" he said thoughtfully, "Wow. It was like the ground just opened up and swallowed us!"

Gribley drew the obvious conclusion, "Master Fintan, sir," he announced, "I believe you have just found your invisible monster!"

THIRTY NINE

A few miles away Mrs Bongo and Suni were attempting to sleep on the rocky slopes of the Nogo Hills. They had followed Fintan's trail all day and been forced to stop when it got too dark to see. The ground wasn't comfortable. In fact it was incredibly uncomfortable, hard and lumpy. Plus, of course, they were hungry, thirsty and exhausted as well as suffering from an assortment of broken bones, sprained muscles and concussion. Mrs Bongo's feet were also horribly swollen and blistered, but that was her own fault for trying to walk in Felicity's sparkly high-heels. A slight mist was drifting down from the higher ground and weird animal noises were echoing through the night air.

"I don't like it up here, Ma," complained Suni, "It's a bit spooky and scary."

His mother rolled over trying to find a less painful spot to sleep on. "Well I don't like it either but you won't hear me moaning about it… so shut up."

Suni didn't want to shut up. He was thinking about all the terrible rumours he'd heard about the Nogo Hills and the invisible monster that lived there. It had to be a pretty enormous beast if it could swallow fifty people at once. It was probably as big as a house. Maybe even bigger! Every little sound he heard made him jump with fright.

"Do you think the monster's real, Ma?" he asked.

"I thought I told you to shut up!" mumbled Mrs Bongo, proving her memory wasn't completely gone, "Go to sleep!"

Half an hour later Suni was still wide awake. The weird animal noises had grown ever louder and so had his mother's snoring. His mind had magnified them all into gigantic, terrifying monsters. A manic, cackling laugh cut through the air just a few metres away. It was the hyenas again. Out there in the darkness their keen sense of smell had picked up the unmistakable scent of warm meat with an added hint of fear. It was a smell they really liked! This particular pack was already in a bit of a funny mood after their recent encounter with Felicity, the human dung-ball. They were feeling hungry and strangely confident.

"Ma," hissed Suni.

His mother continued sleeping and snored like a pig. Something smelly and hairy brushed against Suni's shoulder and drooled slightly on his face.

"Ma!" he squealed, "Wake up, Ma! The monster's here! I think it's going to eat us."

Hyenas, you might remember, don't usually attack humans. It is quite a rare occurrence. They will only do it when they sense that the humans are injured or weak and aren't likely to put up much of a fight. Which is why they decided to jump on Mrs Bongo and Suni and bite them as much as possible.

FORTY

When the sun rose, a shaft of morning light crept into the sink hole and warmed Fintan's sleeping face. He had slept surprisingly well on the cave floor. In fact, apart from a moment in the middle of the night when he had been awoken by the distant cries of hyenas and a lot of screaming, he had slept like a log.

"Good morning, sir," said Gribley who had made a small fire with twigs and was stirring something in a tin can he had saved from the Luxafari picnic, "I trust you slept well?"

"I did thanks, Gribs," said Fintan, sitting up and picking the beetles and worms from his hair, "What are you making there?"

"Moss soup, sir," said Gribley, "I managed to find a small pool of water in the cave and have added some edible bark, lichen and mosses."

Fintan was impressed, "Brilliant," he said.

It wasn't exactly peanut butter on warm toast, but it was better than nothing.

Felicity lifted her head from the heap of debris she was lying on and scowled, "I want to go home, Gribley," she groaned.

She had barely slept at all and was feeling more miserable than she had felt in her whole life, "That was the worst night ever! Why is this ground so uncomfortable?"

She heaved herself up onto one elbow and stretched her aching limbs.

"Ha, look at that, Gribs," blurted Fintan happily, pointing at Felicity's bedding, "She's been sleeping on a skeleton!"

Felicity scrambled to her feet as if her bottom was on fire.

"Oh my God, oh my God, oh my God!" she yelled, frantically brushing a few unidentified lumps of dirt from her dress, "That is *so* disgusting!"

Gribley tried his best to calm the poor girl down while Fintan tried his best not to laugh. Protruding from the mouldering layer of muck on the ground was a complete human skeleton lying awkwardly on its back. Whoever it was must have died there after falling into the hole many years earlier.

"What's that it's holding?" asked Fintan, poking at the clenched bones of the skeleton's right hand, "Looks like a shiny, red rock."

"Interesting," mused Gribley, "I believe the San used a mixture of ground-up coloured stone and animal fat to make their paintings. The poor chap must have been drawing the rock art above when he fell to his death... which explains why the last figure had one very long leg."

"Wow, that's amazing!" breathed Fintan, fascinated at the thought of it, "Can't wait to see what else is down here. Shall we have a proper search after breakfast, Gribs?"

"No, we will not!" objected Felicity loudly, "We're getting out of here and going home right now! Aren't we, Gribley?"

She grabbed her butler by his grubby jacket lapels and stared pleadingly into his eyes, "Get me out of here now, Gribley. I don't want to die in a smelly hole! Actually I don't want to die at all but *especially* not in this smelly hole. And especially not with *him*!"

She glared at her younger brother who was sipping contentedly at his moss soup.

"Ah," said Gribley awkwardly, "I'm afraid I have some rather bad news, Miss Felicity. I have been searching for a way out since first light, but have been unable to find one. We appear to be trapped."

There was a brief pause while Felicity allowed the full impact of this news to sink in. Then the howling began.

"Oh my god, I'm going to die!" shrieked Felicity.

Fintan frowned. This was typical of his sister's selfishness. The truth was they were *all* going to die!

FORTY ONE

The daylight filtering in from above didn't reach far into the cave. To explore the shadows they were going to need some light. Unfortunately Gribley's torch was already out of batteries and Fintan had broken his when they fell. Or possibly before.

"What we need is one of those flaming torches that people use in films," he said rubbing his chin thoughtfully, "You know… a stick with fire on the end like those Egyptologists use for exploring old tombs and stuff."

"Indeed, sir," agreed Gribley, selecting a broken branch from the ground.

"I read a thing in *Young Adventurer* magazine once," continued Fintan, "It was all about this explorer bloke who got lost in the dark somewhere and had to make a flaming torch from things that were lying around."

He screwed up his face trying hard to remember what was involved.

"I think he found a walrus tusk or something and wrapped the end of it in some whale blubber... or was it seal blubber?"

"I see, sir," said Gribley, who was now busy stripping the bark from another fallen branch and bunching it around the end of his stick, "And was this gentleman, by any chance, an Arctic explorer?"

Fintan thought for a moment, "Might've been," he nodded.

"Then may I suggest we try this method instead, sir," suggested Gribley, tying the bark in place with his trouser belt.

Before long, thanks to Gribley's amazing knowledge and Fintan's box of matches, all three of them were equipped with their own fully working flaming torch. Felicity decided she didn't want to carry hers though because it looked really dangerous and she might get sparks on her dress and catch fire.

The first thing they noticed was that the cave was much bigger than they had expected. It stretched off farther than the torchlight could illuminate. The rugged, uneven walls glowed a warm orange colour while weird shadows flickered across their surface. Hundreds more drawings adorned the walls; pictures of animals and humans and strange, horned creatures which looked like a mixture of the two. There were more bones scattered on the ground as well: the remains of long dead creatures which must have fallen into the hole and starved to death in the darkness. There were even bizarre-looking tiny white lizards that skittered blindly around on the ceiling.

"Keep walking, Gribley," muttered Felicity while gripping her butler's free arm, "There *has* to be a way out of this nasty hole!"

In places the cave split into different narrow tunnels which forced them to crouch down or crawl on their hands and knees. Felicity didn't like these bits at all but was terrified of being left behind on her own. Some of the tunnels led nowhere, but others opened out into huge, cavernous chambers decorated with dripping stalactites. Everywhere they went they found more evidence that humans had been there before; more amazing rock art, more abandoned stone tools and butchered animal bones. But still no way out.

"Hey look at that, Gribs!" said a very excited-sounding Fintan, "There's daylight coming in down there!"

It was tiny and barely visible, but there was definitely something bright ahead of them. Fintan led the way. One by one they edged sideways through a very narrow opening in the rock, watching the distant crack of light grow bigger and brighter. After a few minutes of squeezing and struggling they emerged into the fresh air and were hit by a sudden burst of dazzling daylight.

"We're free!" announced a hugely relieved Fintan, shielding his eyes from the glare.

"Well done, sir," said Gribley.

"And about time, too!" moaned Felicity.

But as their eyes adjusted to the light, two things immediately became clear. Firstly, they weren't free at all. They were standing at the bottom of an extremely deep valley with no obvious way out. On either side of them were massive, steep rock faces which looked impossible to climb. They were trapped in a deep gash in the earth like spiders in a giant bath. This was, of course, a bit disappointing.

Secondly though, right in front of them were dozens of human skeletons; some lying on the ground, some propped up against the walls and some which had fallen messily apart. In the centre of this huge mass of bones was a platform constructed from broken branches and rocks which appeared to be some sort of crudely built throne. And sitting on it was another skeleton. This one was wearing a large oval shaped mask carved with geometric patterns and studded with huge diamonds.

Fintan pointed at it, open-mouthed with surprise. Gribley stared in awe and Felicity screamed in terror.

"It's King Zunu!" gasped Fintan.

FORTY TWO

Fintan was overjoyed. Unbelievably, they had found the remains of King Zunu and his legendary lost tribe who had been swallowed by the Nogo Hills monster! OK, so the monster had turned out to be a hole in the ground, which was a bit disappointing, but the diamond-studded mask was real enough! He peered closely at the huge precious stones, marvelling at the way they sparkled in the sunlight.

"This is so brilliant!" breathed Fintan, "I told you we'd find him!"

"Quite astonishing indeed, sir," agreed Gribley.

For a while the two of them stood there side by side, happily examining their discovery. Felicity sat miserably on the dusty ground with her arms folded. Stumbling upon a load of old skeletons in a hole wasn't her idea of a good day out.

"Do you think we should try to take the mask off?" asked Fintan, "So we can see King Zunu's face?"

"That might be a little unwise, sir," cautioned Gribley, "The wood does look rather old and fragile."

He was well aware of the boy's tendency to break valuable objects. There was hardly a vase or statue at home that he hadn't cracked, dropped or knocked out of a window at least once.

"Don't worry, Gribs, I'll be really careful," said Fintan, gently taking hold of the sides of the mask.

Very slowly he lifted it upwards. There was a slight creaking sound and a cloud of dust wafted into the air.

"I really think it would be a good idea to leave it where it is, sir," added Gribley expecting the whole thing to disintegrate at any second.

"It's OK, I've got it," said Fintan confidently, "Look, it's coming off really easily."

It was true. Within seconds, Fintan was proudly holding the mask in his hands and, amazingly, it was completely undamaged. Gribley breathed a sigh of relief.

"Well done, sir!" he said.

Together they gazed upon the face of King Zunu. Or rather, they didn't because he hadn't got one. Unfortunately King Zunu's head had come off, too and was stuck to the back of the mask.

"Oh dear," said Fintan.

There was an odd slurping sound as the skull detached itself from the mask and fell to the ground. Seconds later all the diamonds fell out, too.

"Not to worry," said Fintan, undaunted, "We can probably stick them back in later. Did you bring any glue, Gribs?"

Felicity gave him a round of sarcastic applause, "Typical!" she sneered, "Stupid little brother strikes again! Breaking everything he touches as usual."

Fintan ignored her and gently placed the mask back onto King Zunu's headless skeleton then knelt down and gathered up the fallen diamonds. They were truly enormous and had to be worth a fortune!

"You know what this means, don't you?" he said turning to Gribley and beaming with excitement.

"Of course I do," interrupted Felicity," It means *that's* going to happen to me, too! I'm going to starve to death down this stupid hole and end up a stupid skeleton like them!"

"No, it doesn't. It means we're rich!" said Fintan, attempting to rise above his sister's negative attitude, "It means I can pay back all the money I owe to mum and dad!"

"Oh yeah? And how are you going to do that if you're stuck down here forever?" she snorted.

Gribley tried to sound reassuring. It was part of his job after all.

"Now then, Miss Felicity," he said, "There's no need to worry. I'm sure we'll find a way out sooner or later."

"Well, *they* didn't!" she said, gesturing toward the pile of old bones, "They got stuck down here and died! And they were, like... locals! They were used to this sort of thing! If *they* couldn't find a way out what chance do *we* stand?"

Fintan had to admit it was a worrying thought. What was the point of being fabulously rich if you were trapped in a hole in the middle of nowhere? He didn't admit it out loud, of course. The idea of Felicity being right was just too horrible to contemplate!

But there had to be a way out. He racked his brains for a useful idea. After all, he was an experienced explorer and had been in difficult situations before. Plus he had been reading *Young Adventurer* magazine for years! Surely he must have learned something useful from one of the brilliant articles he had read! After a bit of head-scratching he suddenly remembered the story of the brave Victorian explorer, Captain Fairfax-Doughty. The brave Captain had fallen into an icy crevasse in the Arctic and been trapped there for several days. He had run out of rations and only survived by eating his own gloves. According to *Young Adventurer*, he had eventually escaped by taking off all his clothes, ripping them up and tying the pieces together to make a rope. He had then tied one of his boots to the end, turning it into a makeshift grappling hook, thrown it to the top of the crevasse and hauled himself out. Unfortunately he had frozen to death about ten minutes later, which wasn't surprising as he was completely naked apart from one boot. But that wasn't the point; the point was it was a pretty inspiring story!

"I read this thing once in *Young Adven*—" he began, but was cut off by his miserable sister.

"Oh for heaven's sake!" she snapped." If you say '*Young Adventurer* magazine' one more time I'm going to punch you!"

Fintan paused for a moment before continuing, "There was this explorer bloke called Captain Fairfax-Doughty and he got trapped in a really deep hole just like us—"

Felicity punched him anyway.

"Ow!" said Fintan, rubbing his bruised arm, "Anyway, he didn't have any rope or anything like that and he couldn't get out. So what did he do? He used whatever he could find—"

"Der!" sneered Felicity, "There's no whale blubber down here, you idiot!"

"I'm not talking about blubber this time!" insisted Fintan, "I'm just saying we need to use our resources! We have to ask ourselves 'is there anything down here now that *wasn't* here in King Zunu's time?"

Felicity rolled her eyes in despair and tutted while Fintan rummaged through his bag. He had a street map of Edinburgh, a ball of string, half a box of matches, a broken compass and an empty plastic bottle plus, of course, several huge diamonds bundled up in an empty sausage wrapper. Not exactly the kind of things you needed for climbing out of a deep hole.

"Actually," said Gribley, who had been pondering the question, "We *do* have something which wasn't here before."

Fintan raised a curious eyebrow, "Felicity?" he said uncertainly.

"No, sir, I am referring to King Zunu and his tribe."

Fintan eyed the jumbled pile of skeletons but didn't understand what his butler was suggesting, "But... they're dead," he said.

"Exactly, sir!" agreed Gribley, "We have a large amount of bones with which to build a ladder."

FORTY THREE

Building the bone-ladder turned out to be surprisingly easy. Thigh bones were just right for the vertical parts while arm bones and shin bones made excellent rungs. They couldn't find a use for the smaller bones and rib cages and skulls so Fintan lined them all up on the ground in what he thought was a respectful manner. It was the nearest thing the poor tribe were ever going to have to a funeral. Felicity, of course, decided not to help because she said the old bones were 'icky' and there was 'no way' she was going to touch them.

By early afternoon, the ladder was finished. It wasn't a pretty sight. In fact it looked like something from a horror movie made by nursery school children. Felicity said it was revolting and hideous and that it would probably fall apart as soon as someone stepped on it, but Fintan didn't care. He was very proud of it and especially proud that his ball of string had come in handy for tying all the bones together. Unfortunately, it was nowhere near tall enough to reach the top of the huge valley they were trapped in which meant they were going to have to carry it back through the cave to the sink hole where they fell in. And that meant dismantling it again so it would fit round the bends in the narrow tunnels.

Felicity sat on a rock, enjoying the sight of Gribley and Fintan breaking their newly completed ladder into more manageable pieces. She thought this was really hilarious and laughed a bit more than was actually necessary. Then it was time to retrace their steps through the cave system, but this time, carrying the dismantled ladder. After a short argument, Felicity agreed to carry the wooden mask but only because it was 'much less icky' than the bones. It was a long and difficult journey but eventually the three of them arrived back where they had started.

Fintan and Gribley tied the ladder together again with what was left of the string then hoisted it into position beneath the sink hole. Luckily it was just tall enough to reach the opening which was a relief because there were no bones left. Fintan stepped onto the first rung. It was a bit wobbly but felt surprisingly safe. Very slowly, he began to climb while Gribley held the bottom of the ladder steady.

"Please be careful, sir," he said as the old bones groaned and twisted in his hands.

"It's OK, Gribs," said Fintan reassuringly, "I'll be fine."

Step by creaking step he made his way to the top. Some of the bones slipped out of place and most of Fintan's knots came undone but, amazingly, the ladder held together.

"I made it, Gribs!" he shouted, clambering out into the blinding daylight, "And guess what? There are people up here!"

It was a bit of a weird surprise but standing next to the hole were Mrs Bongo and Suni. Both of them were in a terrible state, which wasn't surprising considering what they had just been through. Over the last couple of days they had been knocked out by rhino-tranquillisers, battered around in a car crash, chased by hungry lions and stuck up a thorn tree all night. They had also crossed a desert with no food or drink and been savaged by a pack of wild hyenas. The younger one's broken arm was sticking out at an alarming angle and so was the older one's bottom.

Fintan recognised them at once. He was amazed. Why had the people from the hotel kitchen followed him all the way out here? Surely they weren't still trying to get their peanut butter back? Were they mad?

"Hello," he said, climbing out of the hole, "What are you two doing here?"

"That's him, Ma," yelled Suni excitedly, "That's the boy who stole our diamonds!"

Mrs Bongo stared quizzically at Fintan. She had definitely seen him somewhere before. A hazy picture began to form in her mind. She was in a large store room and there was a fight going on. Bits of cabbage were flying about and jars were smashing. In the centre of the mess she saw herself wrestling around on the floor while someone with an English accent kept asking for a jar of peanut butter. Abruptly, she remembered exactly who the boy was.

"You!" she snapped, her face reddening with anger, "Where are my diamonds?"

She lunged forward and grabbed him roughly by the throat.

"Pardon?" protested Fintan, "They're not *your* diamonds. They're mine. I found them!"

"No, you didn't," snarled Mrs Bongo, "*We* did! Give them back!"

"Are you all right, Master Fintan, sir?" called Gribley from the bottom of the sink hole.

He didn't like the sound of the angry voices coming from above.

"It's those people from the hotel again, Gribs," shouted Fintan, trying to loosen the woman's grip on his windpipe, "They say they want the diamonds!"

"Really, sir?" said Gribley, "How unfortunate. I shall endeavour to be with you shortly."

"Come on then, give them back!" continued Mrs Bongo, poking Fintan's stomach with her meat cleaver, "They must have come out by now, surely?"

'Come out?' thought Fintan. It seemed like a strange thing to say.

"Er, yes…" he said, wondering how these people knew so much about King Zunu's mask, "They just sort of fell out, actually."

At this point Gribley made it to the top of the ladder and peered out only to find Suni standing over him looking menacing. The youth placed one dirty shoe on Gribley's head and turned back to Fintan.

"Hey, English boy. Hand over the diamonds," he demanded, "Or I'll kick the old man back down the hole!"

Fintan wasn't sure what to do. It seemed really unfair but it appeared he had no choice.

"All right, you can have them." he sighed and delved into his bag for the sausage wrapper full of diamonds.

"Here," he said, handing them over.

Mrs Bongo snatched the package from his hands and peered inside.

"*Oh my God!*" she mumbled, hardly able to believe her eyes.

The diamonds had grown! They were now about ten times bigger than they had been when Fintan swallowed them. Suni quickly joined her to see what she was talking about.

"But how…?" he stammered, "How could this have happened?"

Mrs Bongo had no idea. She turned to Fintan, slack-jawed with amazement, "What did you do to them?" she asked.

Fintan didn't understand the question, "*Do?*" he said, "I didn't do anything to them. Well, I washed them in a puddle, that's all. They were a bit grubby when they came out."

Suni shared an astonished look with his mother. It was a miracle! A bit revolting, but still a miracle. This annoying English boy's digestive system was a thing of absolute wonder that made diamonds grow to unbelievable proportions. Mrs Bongo's mind began to race at the possibilities that lay before them. They could take the boy home, keep him in a cage and make him eat little diamonds. They would go in tiny and come out big! Maybe they could even make him swallow the big diamonds again and wait until they came out the size of pineapples! What this might do to Fintan's bottom wasn't even considered.

While the thieves were distracted by their own greedy imaginations, Gribley climbed out of the hole and pulled Felicity out after him. She blinked in the sudden brightness of the African sunlight and looked hugely relieved to be out of the sink hole. She dumped King Zunu's mask on the ground and took in her surroundings. Then her expression changed. It was those horrible people again! The ones who had ruined their balloon safari and squashed the pilot's handsome face! "What are *they* doing here, Gribley?" she snapped, unable to contain her irritation.

"I'm afraid they are taking King Zunu's diamonds away from your brother, Miss," explained Gribley, "We are being robbed."

Felicity noticed the gloating expressions on the thieves faces as they pawed at the contents of the sausage wrapper. And her blood boiled.

"Please try to remain calm, Miss," suggested Gribley, "These people might be dangerous."

"Remain calm?" she yelled, "Never mind the diamonds; that woman's wearing my dress!"

It was true. Mrs Bongo had squeezed herself into Felicity's favourite silver cocktail dress, which was now ripped, filthy, sweat-stained and had split open at the seams. Felicity was furious. She stormed angrily over to the shameless clothes thief and gave her a good, hard shove.

"Where did you get that from?" she ranted, "Give it back at once!"

Mrs Bongo was taken completely by surprise. She stumbled backwards and fell over. The diamonds spilled from the sausage wrapper and rolled across the ground. At the same time her meat cleaver flew from her hand and sailed through the air. It whizzed past Suni's head, taking a chunk out of his left ear then embedded itself in a tree. The boy shrieked in pain. His ear was one of the few parts of his body that hadn't already been injured.

"Quick, boy, get the diamonds!" yelled his mother, lying awkwardly on her back and failing to be the slightest bit sympathetic.

"OK, Ma," wailed Suni, holding his dangling ear in place with one hand and attempting to gather up the diamonds with his broken arm.

Felicity stared down at Mrs Bongo, sprawled on the stony ground and noticed something even more distressing.

"Oh my God," she squealed, "You're wearing my shoes, too!"

Two conflicting emotions raged through Felicity's mind. She was unbelievably pleased to see her best sparkly shoes again but horrified to see them stretched and battered by Mrs Bongo's lumpy, old feet.

"Give them back you horrid, old witch!" she yelled, then leapt violently onto the woman's legs and attempted to wrench the shoes off her.

The two of them rolled over and over on the dusty ground punching, kicking and throttling each other while Gribley tried to pull them apart.

Fintan watched the chaos in stunned amazement. Everything had got a bit out of control. Then, just when he thought things couldn't get any weirder, the police arrived.

FORTY FOUR

"Police!" announced Inspector Kudu, striding over and holding up his identity badge, "Pack that in at once!

Everyone stopped what they were doing and stared. Mrs Bongo scrambled to her feet and tried to look innocent while Felicity let go of the woman's hair and tried to look sane. Neither of them succeeded. Suni backed away clutching the bag of diamonds wondering where he could hide them. Hurriedly he thrust the diamonds back into Fintan's hands. He didn't want to go to jail.

Parked nearby was a large, dust-covered police car which had somehow made it to the top of the Nogo hills. Weirder still, Mr and Mrs Fedora were climbing out of it along with the no longer handsome pilot.

"So, what's going on here then?" continued the inspector, eying the peculiar, ragged group.

There was so much going on that no one was quite sure where to start.

"Perhaps I can explain?" began Gribley, but was immediately interrupted by a quavering voice from the back of the police car. It was Flavian. He had wound down the rear window and poked his head out.

"That's them!" he yelled, pointing at Mrs Bongo and Suni, "They're the people who attacked me at the hotel!"

Inspector Kudu was taken by surprise; mainly because Flavian hadn't said anything for days.

"What?" he asked, "Are you quite sure?"

"Yes!" said Flavian, nodding vigorously, "The big one sat on my back. I'd recognise that bottom anywhere!"

"And they broke my jaw, too!" added the once handsome pilot but no one understood what he was saying and just nodded politely.

Mrs Fedora rushed over to her daughter and gave her an awkward hug. It would have been a big, emotional hug but Felicity was really dirty and smelled of wild animal dung.

"My poor little girl," sobbed Mrs Fedora, "Are you all right?"

She stroked Felicity's hair tenderly for a moment, then got something nasty stuck to her hand and wished she hadn't. Felicity let out a weak, whining noise. Her mother smelled wonderful! She smelled of perfume and deodorant and civilisation! It meant everything was going to be all right after all! The nightmare was finally over!

"Oh, mum, I knew you'd come!" she wailed, "Take me home. I want to go home!"

All the terrible things she had just been through flashed before her eyes! Her favourite dress was a wreck, her best shoes were ruined and she had deliberately covered herself in dung! And it was all her little brother's fault.

"It was all Fintan's fault!" she bawled, bursting into angry tears and glaring at him with red-faced hatred.

"Wait, what?" said Fintan, "No it wasn't! I only—"

"Look what you've done to your poor sister!" bellowed Mr Fedora, "She's very delicate, you know!"

Felicity nodded in agreement and did her best to look delicate.

"And fancy getting poor Flavian mixed up with these horrible African people!" continued Mr Fedora, "I've never seen the poor boy so upset. He hasn't slept for days! Do you ever stop to think what your silly adventures are doing to your family? Your mother and I have been worried to death these last few days."

"Yeah I know, I'm sorry but it wasn't my fault," objected Fintan.

Mrs Bongo and Suni realised no one was paying them any attention so they slowly edged their way to the back of the group. The Fedora family were far too busy arguing with each other to notice.

"Well, congratulations, young man," continued Mr Fedora sarcastically, "You've done it again. You've completely ruined our whole trip!"

"Fintan always ruins *everything!*" agreed Felicity, nodding her head, "That's exactly what I said to him didn't I, Gribley?"

Gribley nodded sadly, "Indeed you did, miss. Several times."

Inspector Kudu decided he had heard enough arguing and thought he should intervene before people started hitting each other, "Will everybody please be quiet!" he demanded in his best, serious policeman voice, "This isn't helping anyone, now is it?"

The Fedora's obediently shut up and looked like naughty children who had just been told off by a teacher.

"Right then," continued Kudu, enjoying the silence, "Now then, which one of you has the diamonds? Come on, own up."

Everyone looked at everyone else. Fintan looked at his hands.

"Er, I have," he admitted, holding out the sausage wrapper.

This news came as a terrible shock to his parents who gasped in horror and shame. So it was true after all! Their son wasn't just an accident-prone nitwit; he was also a diamond thief!

"In that case," said Inspector Kudu, taking out his handcuffs, "Fintan Fedora, I am arresting you for theft."

Fintan was thoroughly confused, "Theft?" he protested, "But I didn't steal them! I found them, honest I did!"

Mrs Fedora buried her face in her husband's chest and sobbed loudly. Her youngest son was a criminal! Could things possibly get any worse? Once Fintan was safely locked in the cuffs, Inspector Kudu began a careful examination of the evidence. He squinted into the sausage bag and a confused look appeared on his face.

"No, no, no," he said, taking out one of the large, lumpy stones and holding it up to the light, "These aren't Lady Van der Kloot's diamonds. These are *much* too big. Where did you get these, boy?"

"Down there," said Fintan, attempting to gesture towards the sink hole with his handcuffed hands, "They were in King Zunu's mask but they fell out because of woodworm and stuff. I didn't break it on purpose."

"King Zunu's mask?" said the inspector incredulously.

"Yes," said Fintan, "Who's Lady Bandicoot?"

"Never mind that," said the stunned inspector, "Are you telling me that you have found King Zunu's mask?"

Fintan nodded proudly.

"And you found it down that hole?"

Fintan nodded again even more proudly.

"Seriously? You've found the legendary diamond-studded mask of King Zunu? Leader of the lost tribe who were swallowed by the Nogo Hills monster?"

"Yep," said Fintan, "Me and Gribley found it, didn't we, Gribs?"

"And me!" chimed in Felicity, realising she might get the credit for the discovery, and there might even be a reward, "I'm the one who carried it out, see!"

She held up the ancient wooden mask with sudden pride.

The inspector shook his head in disbelief, "Good Lord," he breathed, "That's absolutely incr—"

Suddenly the conversation was drowned out by the loud roaring of an engine. Mrs Bongo and Suni had crept away and were stealing the police car.

"My car!" yelled a startled Inspector Kudu as it sped away in a cloud of dust.

"My son!" added Mrs Fedora.

Flavian was still sitting in the back seat.

FORTY FIVE

"Well, that was unfortunate," mused Inspector Kudu staring at the distant dust cloud, "Very unfortunate indeed."

Considering what an utter disaster it was, he sounded surprisingly calm.

Felicity, on the other hand, was not calm at all. A sudden wave of despair and disappointment swept over her. Just for a moment she had dared to believe the nightmare was finished. But it wasn't. And now the rest of her family were stuck in it, too! She fell to her knees clutching her mother's skirt and sobbed at an unbelievable volume.

"What did I ever do to deserve such a stupid brother?" she howled, while glaring at Fintan, "Why did I have to get dragged into your stupid adventures? And why involve mum and dad and Flavian... and poor old Gribley?"

"I'm here, too," said the used-to-be handsome pilot.

"Whatever," mumbled Felicity.

He wasn't handsome anymore so she'd gone off him. Mr Fedora wasn't staying calm either.

"Now look here!" he began, angrily confronting Inspector Kudu, "You're a policeman aren't you? Our son's in that car with those dreadful people and we want him back, do you hear? I demand to know exactly what you intend to do about it!"

Unfortunately, Kudu said there was nothing he *could* do about it. Not until they got back to civilisation, anyway. His phone had no signal and very little battery while his police radio was in the stolen car. They were just going to have to hope for the best.

"You mean you're going to do nothing to help my poor boy?" wailed Mrs Fedora, "My poor Flavian's been taken by those... those awful... *people!*"

She pointed vaguely in the direction of the disappearing car, "Shouldn't you be following the tyre tracks or something?"

"That won't be necessary, Mrs Fedora," explained Kudu, doing his best to calm her down, "There's nowhere for those people to go except back to the city. Nothing but desert around here for hundreds of miles. Plus I couldn't help noticing that one of them had lost most of her teeth and the other had been missing part of an ear! I imagine they'll be taking themselves straight to the nearest hospital."

Mrs Fedora wasn't convinced, "But aren't they dangerous?" she sniffed, "They looked terrifying!"

"Please try to calm yourself, Madam," continued Kudu, "I'm sure your boy will be quite safe. Those people may *look* dangerous but they probably aren't even armed."

"Apart from that big meat cleaver thing," added Fintan, not very helpfully.

"Shut up, you idiot!" snapped Felicity, punching her brother in the arm.

"Now then," cautioned Inspector Kudu, "Let's not start fighting again! It's vitally important that we all try to be positive, put aside our differences and work together. If we start walking now we should all be safely back at the hotel in a day or so."

Fintan's parents gasped in horror.

"A day or so?" repeated Mr Fedora.

"Walking?" said a distressed Mrs Fedora, who often complained about her sore feet after returning from the hairdressers in the High Street, "From here to the hotel? I can't walk all that way! Not with *my* feet!"

Inspector Kudu was puzzled. Did she want to walk with someone else's feet?

"It'll be all right, mum," said Fintan brightly, "Think of it as an adventure. Might even be fun!"

Mrs Fedora looked at her son with utter disbelief. How had she possibly given birth to such a strange creature? Someone who actually enjoyed being out in the hostile wilderness! All the stress and worry of the last couple of days began to boil over in her mind. Things were falling apart.

"Fun?" she exclaimed, "Let me tell you something, young man. This…" she paused to gesture towards the African wilderness in general, "… is not fun! Trudging around in the hot sun with nothing to eat or drink and with wild animals lurking around every corner waiting to eat me is not *fun*!"

"Sorry," mumbled Fintan again.

"We're all going to die!" wailed Felicity.

FORTY SIX

Luckily the first few miles were all downhill as they gradually descended the other side of the Nogo Hills. Even Mrs Fedora didn't find it too difficult, and she rarely walked anywhere. Conversation turned to the diamond theft. It was obvious now that the real thieves were Mrs Bongo and her weird son and that Fintan was completely innocent. Inspector Kudu apologised for getting everything completely wrong and unlocked the handcuffs. The only remaining mystery was what had happened to Lady Van der Kloot's diamonds. No one, least of all Fintan, had a clue!

After three hours the land flattened out and the rocky terrain changed to savannah. Other than the occasional stunted tree there was nothing but dry, brown grass for miles.

"Just how far from the hotel are we?" asked Mr Fedora, checking his watch and looking very concerned.

Inspector Kudu said he wasn't sure, but it was at least a day and a half away. Everyone groaned. A few more hours passed. The patches of scrubby trees became thicker while the grass became drier, taller and dotted with grazing wildebeest. Felicity didn't like the look of them. She was convinced they were some sort of big, hairy carnivore that was going to eat her, and she had to be calmed down again. Shortly after that, several hopeful vultures joined the group and circled silently overhead. Everyone was gasping for water and Mrs Fedora was complaining about how much her feet hurt. She informed everyone that she had blisters the size of oranges, but no one wanted to see them.

"I tell you what would be good, mum," said Fintan, trying to cheer her up, "Why don't we try and catch one of these wildebeest so you could get a ride on it. Or better still we could catch a zebra or something?"

Felicity groaned but was too weary to argue.

"Seriously," continued Fintan, "They're just like horses only stripier. I read this thing once in *Young Ad*—"

He paused to check whether his sister looked like punching him. As usual she did.

"I read this thing in a magazine once about these people who trained these zebras so they could ride them like horses. Ostriches too! You can ride all sorts of things if you know the right way to do it. I bet I could train one for you, mum. I mean, it can't be that hard, can it? Remember when I trained my hamster to walk a tightrope?"

Mrs Fedora sighed loudly. She remembered it very well. The 'tightrope' had been her washing line and the petrified hamster had pooped all over her clean sheets.

Suddenly the inspector, who was leading the group, stopped and raised his hand for silence. There was a large, unseen animal moving around in the long grass ahead of them. It was making a deep, snuffling noise like some sort of monstrous vacuum cleaner. The erstwhile handsome pilot immediately ducked down out of sight.

"Rhino!" he whispered.

Over the years he'd had plenty of encounters with African wildlife so he knew what he was talking about. Unfortunately no one else did.

"I wonder if it's a zebra?" mused Fintan excitedly, creeping through the undergrowth towards it.

The unhandsome pilot clutched Fintan by the sleeve, "No! It's a rhino, you idiot!" he hissed, "Rhinos are dangerous! They're notoriously unpredictable and can charge at you without warning! Their eyesight isn't very good, but they have excellent hearing and a *really* good sense of smell. For God's sake, leave it alone!"

Fintan pretended to listen patiently and nodded in agreement, "OK," he said, "I'll go and have a look then."

The pilot sighed. The sooner his broken jaw was fixed the better it would be for everyone.

Fintan crouched low, parted the tall grass and advanced slowly towards the hidden creature.

"Don't be a fool, boy," hissed Inspector Kudu, "It might be dangerous!"

"It's OK," explained Fintan calmly, "Animals like me! Well, usually they do anyway. There was this dolphin once that bit me on the bum but only because it was trying to get the fish finger I had in my pocket. I can't remember why I had a fish finger in my pocket now, but that's not the point. The point is I get on really well with animals. You'll see."

Mr Fedora frowned. His son was an idiot. The family clustered together in a frightened clump as Fintan disappeared from view, alone and unarmed. He may be an idiot but he was a brave idiot. Everyone braced themselves for the inevitable sound of trampling hooves, screaming and the splattering of blood, but nothing happened. Moments later they heard Fintan's voice again. He sounded surprisingly happy.

"Oh wow, look at you!" he was saying, "Aren't *you* cute!"

Mrs Fedora, who had been holding her terrified breath, let out a relieved sigh. It wasn't a dangerous animal after all.

"What is it?" she asked as quietly as possible.

"A *baby* rhino!" announced an overjoyed Fintan, "And look at that! His mum's here, too."

The pilot has horrified. It was even worse than he'd thought. A mother rhino could be very aggressive when she had a baby to protect. He closed his eyes and prayed that the boy wouldn't be daft enough to touch the calf.

"There now, that feels nice doesn't it, baby!" said Fintan's cooing voice, "Who doesn't like a good scratch under the chinny chin, eh?"

The non-handsome pilot whimpered to himself. Any second now it was going to be utter carnage!

"Oh you want some attention too do you, Mrs Rhino?" continued Fintan who, much to everyone's surprise, was still alive and still in one piece, "There! Plenty of nice scratches to go around! You're lovely and rough aren't you! Who's a leathery girl with little spiky hairs sticking out, then?"

Now feeling a lot less terrified, Fintan's family slowly emerged from their hiding places. To their amazement, Fintan was patting the mother rhino's head while the calf rubbed happily against his legs.

"So, how do you feel about giving my poor old mum a ride back to the hotel, then?" continued Fintan, as if he was talking to a smiling toddler in a pushchair, "She's got sore feet, she has. Yes! Poor old, sore feet!"

Suddenly the mother rhino looked very alert and on-edge as if she sensed danger.

"Hey, it's OK, there's a good girl," said Fintan soothingly, "They're with me! It just my family and friends!"

He stroked the impressive horn on the rhino's head but she remained nervous and skittish. Fintan couldn't help wondering what on earth she was afraid of. After all, what did a heavily armoured, one thousand kilogram rhinoceros possibly have to be afraid of? Seconds later he found out. There was a snapping noise like someone swatting a fly and mother rhino jerked backwards. Her eyes were wide and her nostrils were flaring. She looked like she was trying to run but had forgotten how. Very quickly she became disoriented and stumbled backwards a few steps while her terrified calf bolted off into the cover of the long grass. Fintan watched, open-mouthed with absolutely no idea what was happening. Then he noticed something strange sticking out of the rhino's neck, which looked oddly familiar. It was one of Mr Bok's tranquilliser darts.

FORTY SEVEN

A few moments later, two heavy trucks came thundering into view. They bounced over the rutted ground, smashed through the trees then stopped in a shower of red dust. A group of men jumped out shouting to each other in an assortment of African languages and surrounded the confused animal. Mother rhino staggered around uncertainly, trying to escape but was quickly subdued and tied around the back legs with sturdy ropes. After a short, hopeless struggle, the tranquilliser dart took full-effect and the huge beast toppled over. Hurriedly the men pushed and pulled her upright and began hauling her up a ramp into one of the trucks.

Fintan didn't like this at all. It seemed very wrong! One minute mother rhino had been standing there with her baby, minding her own business and enjoying a nice grassy lunch, and the next she was being dragged into a truck like a lump of leathery meat! As he stood there feeling helpless, another, smaller vehicle pulled up. Standing confidently in the back was a dirty, bearded man with dark sweaty patches under his arms. It was Henrik Bok.

"Where's the calf?" he shouted to his men sounding extremely angry, "I said I wanted the calf, too! Did you idiots frighten it away?"

No one answered. They all looked a bit scared of their loud-mouthed, sweat-stained boss and continued loading the rhino into a large wooden crate. Then Bok noticed the scruffy boy loitering nearby, looking hopelessly out of place among the African wilderness.

"Who the–?" he sputtered sounding totally puzzled "What are you– where did you just come from, boy?"

Fintan said nothing. There was no short answer to a question like that. And anyway, he really didn't like Mr Bok. The man was rude and cruel and bigheaded and hunted defenceless animals. He was also wearing a pair of khaki shorts which were much too small for him and showed far too much of his hairy legs and knobbly knees.

"Was it you?" continued Bok, gripping his rifle menacingly, "Did you interfere with my hunt?"

Luckily for Fintan, his parents chose that moment to emerge from the bushes behind him looking hugely relieved. Not only did this strange, grubby man speak

English but he had vehicles! They were saved! One by one the others crept out too. Felicity stood between her parents with a huge, weirdly hopeful smile on her dung-smeared face.

Bok was stunned. He stood in the back of his jeep and stared down at the peculiar-looking group. He plonked one dusty boot on the tailgate, rested his rifle on his shoulder and spat into the long grass.

"What the hell are you lot doing out here?" he said arrogantly, "This is no place for you city types. This is the *bush*, man! This is Africa!"

He paused to dramatically wipe the sweat from his forehead.

"This is a dangerous land. It's hard and unforgiving. It's no place for kids and old ladies and… tourists!"

He paused, turned to his men who were struggling to load the rhino, and yelled something insulting in Zulu.

"Yes, well, we're awfully sorry about that." said Mr Fedora trying to sound charming, "The thing is, I was wondering, do you think you could possibly give us a lift back to town? I mean if it's not too much bother?"

"We're staying at the Hotel Impala," added Mrs Fedora, who didn't want to walk any further than she really had to.

Bok took a lengthy swig from his water bottle then wiped his mouth with his sweaty hand.

"Thought as much," he crowed, nodding to himself, "Can't take it out here, can you? Want to go back to the big city, eh?"

"Yes please," replied Felicity and her parents in unison.

Bok jumped casually down from the back of his jeep and began swaggering around. He was really enjoying his big chance to show off.

"OK, I'll take you," he said after a bit of pacing, "But I warn you it's going to be rough. This isn't first class travel with reclining seats and all that rubbish. You'll have to ride in the back with the animals."

Fintan's parents and sister exchanged a horrified look. This didn't sound very comfortable at all, but if it meant not having to walk they were prepared to put up with it.

"Thank you very much," grinned Mr Fedora.

"Most kind of you," said Felicity.

Once the rhino was safely locked up in the crate it was time for the convoy of vehicles to depart. There were seven trucks in all, each carrying various sized wooden boxes loaded with drugged animals. The drivers got into their cabs and started their engines while the rest of the men climbed aboard an open backed lorry and stood waiting to go. Then the negotiations began. Somehow they had to decide who got to ride where. Admittedly it was more like 'shouting and bickering' than 'negotiation' but it was quickly agreed that Mrs Fedora should sit in the front with Mr Bok. Her husband and Inspector Kudu agreed they would ride with Bok's gang of men even though it meant having to stand up all the way. The hitherto handsome pilot was going to have to share with four sedated wildebeest while Gribley was allocated a small space in a box full of zebras. Felicity, despite begging to be allowed a proper seat, was told she had to share a crate with ten sleeping warthogs. And she wasn't happy about it.

"But," she protested, "What about the smell?"

"It's all right, they won't mind," said Fintan.

Felicity fumed. This was yet another injustice she wasn't going to forget about. Once they got back to civilisation her little brother was going to pay dearly for everything he had said and done. Finally Mr Bok stared at Fintan wondering where to put him. He looked puzzled.

"I know you don't I, boy?" he said, scratching his straggly chin, "Where have I seen you before?"

Fintan decided that telling the truth at this point would probably be a bad idea. If he admitted losing the man's hunting gear, stealing most of his tranquilliser darts and ruining his zebra hunt from a hot air balloon he might not get a lift after all. He shrugged his shoulders and tried to look innocent.

"Don't know," he said.

Bok wasn't sure why but he didn't like the look of Fintan so he decided to put him in with the rhino. Fintan was relieved. At least he wasn't sharing with the crocodiles.

FORTY EIGHT

Mrs Bongo's driving wasn't very good. Despite being in some of the emptiest terrain on earth she had somehow managed to scrape the stolen police car against every available boulder, tree and wildebeest on the way. The car was a mess of dents, scratches and dung, and all the suspension springs were broken. Suni could see the ground rushing by beneath his feet where a concrete-hard termite mound had ripped out half the floor. If his mother had known how to use the steering wheel properly she might have avoided some of the collisions, but most of the time she just ploughed randomly forwards. Also, if she had known how to use the rear view mirror properly she might have seen the terrified person crouching down on the back seat!

Flavian couldn't believe they hadn't noticed him yet. He was lying on his side, facing the back with his knees up and his arms covering his head. And he was terrified.

He was fully aware that the woman driving the car carried a meat cleaver the size of a machete and was very likely to use it. It was only a matter of time before she spotted him and chopped him into little pieces!

The woman's navigation skills were no better, either. She had driven around in circles for the first couple of hours with absolutely no idea where she was going before accidentally finding a rough dirt-track crossing their path.

"Which way do we go, Ma?" asked Suni, "Left or right?"

His mother had no idea. Her memory was almost completely back to normal now but it was no help in situations like this. African dirt-tracks all looked pretty much the same and either direction could lead absolutely anywhere.

"How should I know?" she grumbled, "Why don't *you* try making a decision for once?"

Suni wasn't good at decisions. He found them a bit scary. Probably because his mother always yelled at him when he got something wrong. Then again, she also yelled at him when he got something right so it was much easier and safer to let her decide everything.

"OK," he said and reluctantly got out of the vehicle.

He stood in the middle of the dirt-track, staring around for some helpful sign of civilisation. There was nothing. Just endless savannah, grass and dust in all directions. If he had known how to calculate north from the position of the sun in the sky he might have had a clue, but Suni knew nothing of the sort. His education had mostly involved avoiding lessons, stealing things and punching people. It was no help at all.

"Well?" called his mother's rasping voice from the car.

"Dunno, Ma," he said, "Could be that way... or maybe? No, wait..."

Mrs Bongo's patience ran out. There hadn't been much of it there in the first place. She sighed, got out of the car and stomped over to her son. He took a step or two backwards expecting a walloping.

"Stand still," she ordered.

She grabbed him by the shoulders, spun him round three times then let go. Suni wobbled a bit, feeling confused and giddy.

"That way," announced his mother, looking in the direction that Suni's broken arm was pointing.

FORTY NINE

Further ahead on the same track, Mr Bok's convoy of vehicles was making its way towards the city. The journey was long, bumpy and uncomfortable. The crates were cramped, dark, smelly and alive with irritating flies. Felicity cried most of the way. It was only the thought of doing horrible, revenge related things to her little brother that kept her going.

Fintan, however, really enjoyed the trip. It was an amazing opportunity to spend some quality time with a massive, sleeping rhinoceros; something most people never get the chance to do. Mother rhino looked a very sorry sight. She was completely groggy, sitting like the sphinx propped up in a scattering of grubby straw. He stroked her harsh, lumpy skin, waved the flies away from her eyes and, even though she couldn't hear him, talked to her all the way back. He decided to call her Gertie after one of his elderly aunties who, like the rhino, was really wrinkly and had a very similar smell. He also decided that as soon as he got a chance he was going to set her free. She had a calf out there in the bush, all on its own! It wasn't fair to lock up a mother in a zoo while her baby was left behind! He had no idea how he would do it, but he knew it had to happen.

FIFTY

Back in the stolen police car, Mrs Bongo was finally getting the hang of driving. The dirt-track was mostly a straight line and a lot less rutted than the surrounding country so she hadn't hit anything for ages. Even more amazingly, Flavian was still managing to hide in the back seat. After another hour of bumping and jolting, Suni suddenly spotted something in the road ahead.

"Ma, look!" he blurted, "Stop the car!"

Ahead of them, wandering around, looking lost, was a baby rhino. There was no sign of its mother anywhere. Mrs Bongo, whose concussion had mostly worn off, remembered that baby rhinos were worth money; lots of money, if you could find the right buyer! This was an opportunity not to be missed!

She stamped hard on the brake pedal. The car stopped so abruptly that everyone was thrown forwards. Suni head-butted the windscreen while his mother plunged into the inflating airbag. Flavian shot off the back seat and thumped painfully into the front ones. None of them were wearing seat belts. The baby rhino stopped, too. It stared curiously at the filthy, wrecked vehicle hoping it might contain his lost mother, and made a plaintive mewling sound. Suni fell back into his seat clutching his bloody nose while his mother disentangled herself from the air bag. Flavian, seeing this as his chance to escape, flung open the car door and ran for it. Mrs Bongo was stunned in more ways than one.

"Did you see that?" she panted, "Who was that?"

Suni was more concerned with the sharp pain in his nose which had at least taken his mind off the pain in his ear and his broken arm.

Mrs Bongo opened her door. There was a gangly, uncoordinated white boy running away as fast as he could. He had apparently just emerged from the back of the car.

"Hey!" she shouted, "Hey you!"

Flavian glanced back, expecting a razor sharp meat cleaver to come flying towards him at any moment, then stumbled and tripped. He fell face first onto the bone-dry, lumpy ground.

"Where did you come from?" hollered a mystified Mrs Bongo.

The boy sat up and shuffled backwards on his bottom, looking utterly petrified, "Don't kill me!" he squeaked.

Mrs Bongo had no idea what he meant. She had no memory of ever seeing him before, let alone of trying to kill him! Unless, of course, the boy was talking about her terrible driving? At that moment, to everyone's surprise, the baby rhino trotted over to Flavian and sniffed him with great enthusiasm. He smelled just like that other boy who had stroked him earlier. Flavian was now the nearest thing the little calf had to a mother.

Unfortunately Flavian didn't like animals. They had a habit of wanting to sit on his lap or lick his face, which he couldn't stand because it messed up his clothes and interfered with his moisturiser.

"Get away!" he shrieked, trying to shuffle further backwards, "Shoo!"

The happy little rhino ignored his protests, climbed onto his lap and snuggled down for a nap. Mrs Bongo was delighted. The rhino liked the boy. It would make the valuable beast much easier to catch!

FIFTY ONE

It was dark by the time the convoy of vehicles arrived back at Hotel Impala. Everyone piled out, exhausted, aching and filthy. Bok's men walked off into the night to catch their buses home while everyone else headed into the hotel.

Felicity dashed up to her room and plunged straight into the shower. It was the best one she'd ever had, despite the drain clogging up with lumps of dung. Mr and Mrs Fedora followed Inspector Kudu to the nearest telephone and waited while he made an urgent call to the police station. A missing person report was filed and a search party was sent out to rescue Flavian from his captors. The not very handsome pilot, meanwhile, took a fistful of painkillers and called himself a taxi to the hospital. Gribley wished everyone goodnight and disappeared into his room for a long overdue sleep. Once Bok had finished checking all the padlocks on the animal crates he went and sat in the hotel bar where he immediately ordered three very large whiskeys; all for himself.

Fintan was exhausted. He let himself into his room, crumpled onto his bed and spent a while in deep thought. Once again his expedition had been a brilliant success; another triumph for fearless Fintan, the intrepid boy-explorer! So why wasn't he feeling happy? King Zunu's mask was an amazing discovery and one that he was really pleased with but something was bothering him. He took the mask from his bag, propped it up on the bedside table and admired it. Even without its diamonds it was still a fabulous sight. He decided he would fix it in the morning as soon as he found some glue, or failing that, some chewing gum. It would be worth a fortune to the antiquities museum and he'd be rich!

The trouble was he couldn't stop thinking about Gertie. Poor Gertie, locked up in the car park waiting to be shipped to some zoo or other. She was going to be stuck in a cage and be gawped at by people for the rest of her life. And what about Gertie's baby? Abandoned out there in the dark; defenceless and alone among all those lions and hyenas and things. He had to do something.

He made his way back to the ground floor and walked out to where the trucks were parked for the night. The door to Gertie's crate was tightly shut and padlocked. There were deep, rumbling breaths coming from inside. He had no idea how long a dose of tranquilliser lasted on a rhino but he remembered reading something in *Young Adventurer* once which said it was harmful if animals were left sedated for too long. He was just going to have to talk to Mr Bok and persuade him to let Gertie go.

It didn't take long to find Bok. He was in the bar, sprawled in the same leather armchair as before, and he was blind drunk. The table in front of him was covered in empty whisky glasses. His eyes were red and droopy and he stank of sweat and booze.

"Excuse me, Mr Bok," began Fintan awkwardly, "Can I have a word please?"

The drunk man gazed up at him trying to focus.

"Who are you?" he slurred, then belched out a stomach-full of very stinky gas.

Fintan introduced himself while fanning the revolting smell away from his face.

"I've come to ask you a favour," he said, "Can you let the rhino go please? She's got a baby and—"

"Wait! I know *exactly* who you are," interrupted Bok, pointing a dirty finger at him, "You're that boy who hates zoos aren't you! It's all coming back to me now!"

Fintan nodded proudly, folded his arms and looked very serious.

"You're that idiot boy that packed my gear in the truck and lost half of it!" continued Bok, getting increasingly agitated.

"Thing is, you see, she's got a baby rhino out there and—"

Bok wasn't interested.

"I bet it was you who stole my tranquilliser darts, too!" he barked, "Thought you could stop me catching anything, didn't you! Thought you were saving all those poor little fluffy animals from the zoo! Well, I showed you, didn't I!"

He paused, chucked another glass of whiskey down his throat, then laughed an ugly triumphant laugh.

"Interfering little dumkop!" he sneered, "What the hell did I give *you* a lift back for? Should've left you out there for the jackals."

Fintan bit his lip furiously. There was a surge of something very unpleasant welling up inside him which felt like anger. He tried to think of something really insulting to say back but he wasn't very good at that sort of thing.

"Oh yeah, well…you stink!" he observed.

Bok had been waiting for an excuse to hit the boy and this seemed to be it. He levered himself out of his chair, rose drunkenly to his feet and swung his clenched fist in Fintan's direction. Luckily he was so drunk that he missed completely and fell face-first onto the glass-topped table. An empty whisky bottle was launched into the air and came down hard on the back of his head.

The barkeeper rushed over to see what all the commotion was.

"I think you've had enough to drink, sir," he suggested to the man lying on the floor in a mess of blood, broken glass and spilled whiskey, "You should probably go up to bed."

There was no reply apart from a low moaning sound. Between them the barkeeper and Fintan helped Mr Bok to his feet. He was a complete mess and didn't seem to know where he was.

"It's all right," said Fintan smiling happily, "I'll help him up to his room."

FIFTY TWO

Five minutes later Fintan was back outside in the car park but this time he was carrying a large bunch of keys which he had found dangling on Mr Bok's belt. He checked to make sure no one was around then went from vehicle to vehicle unlocking all the crates. He lowered the ramp at the back of Gertie's truck and stood back expecting her to bolt past him. But nothing happened. She just lay there twitching her ears a bit.

"Come on, girl," he coaxed, but she still didn't move.

In his imagination the hard bit of the plan had been finding a way to unlock the crates and he had done that bit really easily. He hadn't expected *any* difficulty persuading the animals to leave them! However, every one of them just lay there, barely awake, and ignored their wide open doors to freedom. Fintan wasn't sure what to do. Gertie was far too heavy to shove so he decided to start with something smaller.

Unfortunately he had never read anything in *Young Adventurer* magazine about how to wake up tranquillised warthogs. First he tried stroking them, scratching their heads and rubbing their noses. It didn't work. He leant against their rumps and shoved. He tried whispering "wake up" in their ears but that didn't help either. They were just too heavily drugged.

It took about an hour of pushing, shoving and cajoling before any of them moved at all. Finally one of the warthogs got to its feet and swayed around a bit.

Fintan encouraged it to venture outside until it tottered unsteadily down the ramp. After this, the others were a little bit easier.

"Off you go then," said Fintan.

But they didn't. Instead of bounding gratefully away, the warthogs just stood there looking confused.

"Go!" urged Fintan quietly while waving his arms about, "Shoo! You don't want to be locked up in a zoo for the rest of your life do you?"

It was the same with all the other animals, too. The zebras, the wildebeest and the gazelles were all incapable of wandering away. Even when he dragged the crocodiles out of their crate they were reluctant to leave the car park. Some animals only made it as far as the nearby bushes then lay down and went back to sleep. By this time two more hours had gone by and Fintan was utterly exhausted. Reluctantly he decided that he had done all he could do. He closed all the crates and clicked the padlocks back on.

All that was left was Gertie. She was just standing there, looking all forlorn and lost. Fintan could tell she wanted to run but all she could manage was a slow shuffle before sitting down again.

"Come on, girl," pleaded Fintan, "You have to go home!"

Gertie staggered the wrong way across the car park with her eyes half closed and bumped into a wall. This wasn't good. She was right outside the hotel's front door and fully illuminated by an exterior light.

"Not that way!" insisted Fintan, "They'll see you! You have to go home."

He pointed across the car park, past the traffic lights and distant shopping centre, towards the freedom of the African plains. It was a long way off and Gertie didn't appear to be in a fit state to get there. She just wanted to sleep. No matter how much Fintan explained the situation to her, she stayed put and stumbled about on her very tired looking legs. A change of plan was needed. He was going to have to hide her for the night and hope that she felt better in the morning. On either side of the hotel entrance were some massive terracotta pots overflowing with decorative flowering plants. Gertie was right next to one of them so he tried his best to get her to lie down behind it. At that moment the hotel's automatic doors slid open and a man in a business suit walked out looking a bit drunk.

"Good evening," he slurred, lifting his hat politely, "Or is it morning? I have no idea."

"Hello," said Fintan, quickly standing in front of Gertie as if it would hide her from sight.

The man smiled and tottered off into the darkness. For a moment he thought he had just seen a scruffy young English boy trying to shove a rhino behind an ornamental flower pot, but blamed it on drinking too many glasses of wine. Fintan smiled back awkwardly as the man disappeared into the night. Unfortunately, when he turned around again it was just in time to see Gertie wandering into the hotel reception.

Horrified at what might happen next, Fintan hurried inside. Luckily the receptionist was glued to her computer screen and hadn't noticed the enormous rhino attempting to check in. Gertie trotted clumsily across the polished floor towards a comfy seating area. Fintan dashed over and steered her away from the beautiful white sofa before she had a chance to smear it with mud. Then she changed course and blundered into a low coffee table, knocking over a carved wooden Zulu head which Fintan had to dive headlong to catch before it clattered onto the floor. He placed it back on the table, carefully steadied a tottering vase of flowers then attempted to turn Gertie around. It was no good. She insisted on continuing across the reception all the way to the far wall.

"Can I help you at all?" asked the receptionist suddenly looking up.

Judging by the relaxed look on her face she couldn't see the rhino, which was now sniffing a potted plant by the lifts. Fintan forced his mouth to make a nervous smile. It was probably the most unconvincing one he'd ever done.

"Er, no, I'm fine thanks," he wittered, "Just been out for a little midnight stroll, you know, er... bit of exercise... fresh air. I'm not up to no good or anything!"

He glanced towards the rhino which was now busy dropping some fresh dung onto a fancy tribal rug.

"Ooh, look over there!" he said pointing in the opposite direction at nothing in particular.

The receptionist looked but failed to see anything unusual.

"What?" she said.

"Er… shooting star," said Fintan, improvising as best he could, "Thought I saw one… outside."

Amazingly the receptionist still hadn't seen the rhino, but it was only a matter of time before she smelled it. A short, pointless conversation followed about how nice it was to see a shooting star and how they didn't happen very often, did they? Fintan nodded and smiled a lot but wasn't listening. He leant on a pillar trying to look casual, while continually glancing towards Gertie. The fourth time he looked she was gone. And the lift door was closing.

"Anyway," said Fintan, suddenly stretching his arms out and pretending to yawn, "It's past my bedtime. I'd better be off."

He walked swiftly over to the lift while the receptionist wished him good night and went back to her computer screen. Fintan pressed the 'call-lift' button and waited for it to come back down. When the doors opened it was empty apart from a little more dung. There was no sign of Gertie. Panicking, he hurried inside and dragged the rug in after him, complete with its steaming pile of rhino poo. Once the doors had closed he quickly gathered all the mess onto the rug and crumpled it into a large, stinking ball. He had to get rid of it somehow.

Back at her desk, the receptionist's nostrils started to twitch. There was a very unpleasant stink in the air. She looked around suspiciously, then checked the soles of her shoes in case she had trodden in something. There was nothing there. She concluded it must have been that odd boy who had just left. No wonder he dashed off in such a hurry!

Fintan got out at the next floor, found a cupboard full of freshly laundered sheets and stuffed the soiled rug inside. It wasn't a very good hiding place but it would have to do. He had a rhino to find!

As it turned out, finding a rhino in a hotel wasn't actually that difficult. All he had to do was follow the series of rhino foot-shaped dents in the carpet and the muddy smears on the wallpaper. The trail weaved around for a while then stopped at room 15. It was Mr Bok's room. And the door was wide open. Fintan must have forgotten to close it when he had helped the drunken man up to bed.

Cautiously he tiptoed inside. Bok was lying face down on his bed, fully dressed apart from his trousers which he had somehow managed to remove and drop on his bedside lamp. Other than that, he was exactly where Fintan had left him, stinking of whiskey and snoring like a walrus with a snotty nose. At the far end of the room, a very similar snoring sound was coming from the bathroom. Fintan crept towards it and peered around the door. It appeared Gertie had found herself somewhere safe to sleep for the night. It was possibly the worst place in the whole hotel she could have chosen but there was nothing he could do about it.

'Oh well,' he thought to himself, quietly closing the bathroom door, 'At least I tried.'

He returned Bok's bunch of keys to his belt and snuck out of the room.

FIFTY THREE

The following morning, Fintan got up surprisingly early. He had slept really well but been woken by a strange feeling in his stomach which had grown increasingly urgent. No matter how much he wanted to ignore it and stay in the nice comfy bed he really needed to get up and go to the loo. It was long overdue after all.

About an hour later when he finally emerged from the toilet, Gribley had arrived and was laying out clean clothes for the day.

"Hey, Gribs," announced Fintan with a big smile on his face, "Look what I just found in the loo; some tiny diamonds!"

He held out a handful of small, sparkling stones, "I told you they were lying around all over the place in South Africa, didn't I!"

Gribley was intrigued. South Africa was, indeed, famous for its diamonds, but they were usually found deep underground in diamond mines. They didn't just turn up in people's toilet bowls. And anyway, these were 'cut' diamonds; ones that had been shaped and polished by a jeweller, not the natural, rough ones that were found in the earth.

"Fascinating, sir," he said, working through the idea in his mind, "Pardon me for asking but was this your first visit to a lavatory for some time?"

"Yeah, first time in ages actually," smiled Fintan, "It was probably that big jar of peanut butter that bunged me up."

"Peanut butter, sir?" enquired Gribley, raising both eyebrows.

This was the first he had heard of it. After a little in-depth questioning, Fintan was persuaded to explain the whole story; his unpleasant encounter with Mrs Bongo and son in the kitchen, how he had eaten a whole jar of 'really crunchy' peanut butter and the stomach ache it had given him. Finally Gribley understood exactly what had happened. These were Lady Van der Kloot's missing diamonds. Mrs Bongo and Suni must have stolen them, hidden them in the peanut butter and had been trying to get them back ever since. All this time Fintan had been walking around with a million rand's worth of diamonds in his belly!

"Master Fintan, sir," he said, "May I suggest we give these diamonds a very thorough wash. I believe there is a handsome reward for their return!"

FIFTY FOUR

Inspector Kudu received an early morning phone call from one of his colleagues. It sounded like good news. His stolen police car had been found. Not only that, but it had been found right outside the Hotel Impala! He was immediately driven to the spot, accompanied by three big, burly policemen armed with serious-looking guns. They leapt from the car pointing their weapons at anything that moved and slowly approached the abandoned vehicle.

It was a mess. It had been parked half in the road and half on a flower bed and looked like it had been driven through every ditch, pothole and swamp for a hundred miles and scraped against an infinite number of trees, rocks and other vehicles. Both the front doors were wide open and there was no sign of the thieves.

However, sitting rigidly in the back seat was Flavian Fedora. He was staring straight ahead in silent shock, trembling slightly and in an even worse state than the car. Stranger still, there was a baby rhino asleep on his lap.

FIFTY FIVE

A short while later Fintan and Gribley went downstairs, ready for the best breakfast they'd eaten in days. Fintan was carrying the newly glued together Mask of Zunu while Gribley had Lady Van der Kloot's freshly scrubbed diamonds in a small plastic bag. It was time to exchange both items for some very big rewards!

The hotel's large, fancy dining room was full of people enjoying their large, fancy breakfasts. Fintan spotted his parents and went to sit with them. They were involved in a very serious conversation with Felicity regarding the possible whereabouts of poor Flavian. Mrs Fedora was worried sick, sobbing softly and already on her third box of tissues. Felicity looked exhausted and was already on her third cup of coffee.

"Morning," said Fintan cheerfully, taking a seat next to his mother.

She briefly glanced at him the way a tired old dog looks at an annoying puppy.

"Hello," she sighed.

"Has there been any news of Master Flavian?" enquired Gribley.

"Not yet," said Mr Fedora, looking at his watch "We're waiting for a phone call. The inspector said he'd be calling us first thing. No word yet."

"What did you bring that thing down for?" sneered Felicity pointing at the diamond-studded mask in Fintan's hands, "Showing off again?"

"Actually I suggested he bring it, miss," explained Gribley, hoping to head off another unpleasant argument, "I have arranged for a gentleman from the local museum of antiquities to come and examine it. I hear he is very excited about the discovery and may wish to purchase it."

Felicity looked unusually interested, "Really?" she asked, wide-eyed with anticipation, "How much am I getting for it?"

Before Gribley could reply he was interrupted by Mrs Fedora jumping to her feet and letting out a shriek of joy. Inspector Kudu had just walked into the dining room, and staggering alongside him was her long lost son.

"My Flavian!" she gasped, "You're alive! My boy's alive!"

The shell-shocked boy was escorted to the table where he was met with a barrage of hugs, kisses and questions, none of which he seemed able to respond to. A waitress poured him a large cup of coffee which he held in both trembling hands and sipped as if it was the most delicious thing in the world.

Inspector Kudu explained that the stolen police car had been found just outside the hotel where the thieves had dumped it before disappearing. He pointed to the window where there was a clear view of the wrecked car. Everyone craned their necks to get a good look. Kudu said that it had been left there sometime during the night so Flavian had probably been sitting in it for hours. The one thing no one could explain, however, was why he had been found holding a baby rhino. Presumably Flavian knew the reason but he was in no state to explain.

At that moment Gribley spotted Lady Van der Kloot shuffle into the dining room closely followed by the man from the museum. He excused himself and went over to ask them to join the Fedora family's table. More happy reunions followed. Lady Van der Kloot was overjoyed to be reunited with her cherished diamonds again, and the man from the Museum of Antiquities was absolutely stunned to find himself holding the legendary mask of Zunu.

Fintan's exploits as an explorer were loudly praised and a small crowd of hotel guests gathered around to marvel at his discoveries. Everyone made a big fuss over him and said complimentary things. Both the inspector and Lady Van der Kloot apologised to him for ever thinking he might have been a suspect. They said that, on the contrary, he was obviously a very honest and capable young man. Felicity really hated that bit.

Fintan was feeling pretty pleased with himself. He felt the morning was going extremely well. In fact it felt pretty close to perfect! The family were reunited, Lady Van der Kloot had her diamonds back and the museum had a fabulous new artefact to display. Also he had been found innocent of theft, hailed as a great explorer and was holding an astonishing amount of reward money. Best of all though, he had freed Gertie and the other animals from captivity! He had no idea where any of them had gone but at least they were no longer in those horrible crates. Things had worked out astonishingly well!

"Here you are, dad," announced Fintan, handing over the massive wad of money, "I said I'd pay you back, didn't I?"

FIFTY SIX

Meanwhile upstairs Henrik Bok found himself rudely awoken by a peculiar sound. There were snuffling noises coming from his bathroom. He sat up in bed, a bit too quickly, and immediately regretted it. He had the worst headache ever. A sudden searing pain flashed behind his eyes and the contents of his stomach fizzed like a shaken bottle of vinegar. Drinking most of a bottle of whisky tended to do that to a person.

The annoying noises got gradually louder and more frequent until they became an intolerable thumping din. Bok felt dreadful, but somehow he had to make the noises stop. Moving very tentatively, in case his brain sloshed about inside his skull, he slid his legs out of bed and tried to put on his slippers. To his surprise he was still wearing his boots from the night before and was fully dressed apart from his shorts which had disappeared.

"Shut up, will you!" he moaned through clenched teeth and limped gingerly across the room.

As he approached the bathroom door he heard another thump and what sounded like breaking glass. The sharp sound vibrated through his fragile head and made him wince.

"This is not funny!" he moaned, and threw open the door.

He really had no idea who might be in there but what he found took him completely by surprise. There was an adult female rhinoceros in his bathroom and she looked very angry. She was tossing her head and snorting and appeared to have broken everything in sight. The shower curtain had been ripped to pieces and parts of it were trailing from the terrifying horn on her head. She had smashed the washbasin off the wall and destroyed the bathtub. Water was gushing out from several broken pipes and flooding the floor. Bok stood there rooted to the spot in terror. Then the rhino charged.

FIFTY SEVEN

Back downstairs in the dining room, Fintan's perfect morning was still feeling pretty perfect. Even the occasional muffled thud from above didn't spoil his good mood and when Felicity started complaining about water dripping onto her face it was just one more thing to be happy about. Unfortunately, things were about to get very weird.

It started when he noticed two suspicious looking people standing at the back of the crowd. They were wearing the worst disguises in the world in a pathetic attempt to blend in. The older one, a woman with an abnormally large bottom and very few teeth, was dressed in a heavy fur coat, heart-shaped sunglasses and the sort of plastic jewellery that little girls dress up in. The younger one was wearing a stripy green suit with a bright orange flowery tie and a baseball cap pulled down over his eyes. His nose was red and swollen to the size of a satsuma while one of his ears was held on with sticky tape. Both of them were staring intently at the mask, the diamonds and the reward money. The woman was visibly drooling.

Fintan resisted the urge to stand up and point at them in case it made things worse. Instead he gave Gribley a little kick under the table and tilted his head discreetly towards them. Gribley recognised them, too. He also recognised that this was a job for the police and not for underpaid butlers. He had no intention of confronting these meat cleaver-wielding lunatics ever again. He gave a very slight cough to get Inspector Kudu's attention.

"Are you all right?" enquired Kudu, wondering why he was being stared at so oddly.

Gribley and Fintan both did a little head nod suggesting that the inspector take a glance over his shoulder. Kudu glanced back, saw the badly disguised pair and immediately knew what to do. His years of experience in the South African police had trained him how to handle delicate situations like this so that nobody got hurt. Carefully he slid his police radio from his jacket and made a brief, whispered call. The armed policemen posted outside were notified that the suspects, Mrs Bongo and Suni were in the building and preparing to make a grab for the diamonds again. They loaded their guns and moved into position.

"There it is again!" moaned Felicity, "I'm telling you! There's definitely water dripping on me!"

Her mother was irritated, "Is that all you can think of to talk about?" she complained, "Your poor brother has just been returned to us after a terrible ordeal which was so unbelievably awful that it has rendered him speechless and you're moaning about a few drops of water!"

"It's not just a few drops!" protested Felicity, looking upwards, "Look, there's a big dark stain on the ceiling! I bet it's a leaking tap or something."

But no one was looking. Instead everyone's attention was focussed on a sudden commotion going on at the back of the dining room. A tubby, soaking wet businessman wearing nothing but his swimming trunks was running between the tables and screaming in terror.

"There are crocodiles in the swimming pool!" he screeched, "They tried to eat me!"

The hotel's brochure had said nothing about the possibility of crocodiles in the pool and he was very unhappy about it. Running blindly forwards he collided with a waitress who had been carrying a large tray loaded with steaming hot bacon and eggs which splattered into the lap of a waffle salesman from Belgium. The waffle salesman let out a shrill cry of pain and jumped up knocking his chair backwards.

"I demand to see the manager!" continued the man in swimming trunks who was now sprawled on the floor, covered in baked beans.

Mrs Bongo and Suni saw this noisy diversion as their big chance. While everyone was looking the other way they shoved through the crowd to the Fedora's table, knocking Flavian off his chair in the process. Suni grabbed the wad of reward money, stuffed it into his pocket, then snatched the diamond mask. Meanwhile his mother produced a large meat cleaver from inside her coat. The assembled crowd gasped and drew back a little. Waving her cleaver Mrs Bongo forced a path to where Lady Van der Kloot was sitting and reached for the little bag of diamonds.

"Oh no you don't!" snapped Lady Van der Kloot, clutching the diamonds to her bosom and punching Mrs Bongo in the face.

It was a really good punch, too. Mrs Bongo dropped to the floor like a bag of bowling balls and lay there staring cross-eyed at the ceiling. Inspector Kudu rolled her over, wrenched her arms behind her back and slapped on a pair of handcuffs. She was finally under arrest! Suni wasn't sure what to do. Should he make a run for it with the loot or stay and help his lovely mother escape? It didn't him take long to decide. Within a second he was sprinting for the door like a frightened rabbit. Unfortunately for him it was just in time to meet three heavily armed policemen on their way in.

"Get down!" demanded the first policeman, pointing his rifle at Suni's head.

"On the floor now!" added the second one just in case the youth hadn't understood.

Suni had understood perfectly. He emitted a high-pitched squeak and dropped to the carpet. The policemen gathered around him levelling their guns and yelling orders for him not to move. The third policeman knelt on the boy's back and clicked on the handcuffs, which wasn't easy as one of his arms was pointing the wrong way. The drama was all over! The assembled hotel diners had never experienced a breakfast like it.

"This place has gone mad!" muttered the boring man from Croydon, with a half-eaten sausage poised on his fork, "Makes you wonder what's going to happen next, doesn't it!"

What happened next was even madder. There was a thunderous creak from overhead which caused everyone to look up. The dark patch on the ceiling had grown to an enormous size and was sagging like an overweight pig's belly.

"I told you there was a leak, didn't I!" insisted Felicity.

As she spoke, a jagged line split the dark patch from end to end, and hundreds of litres of water poured through the crack. Inspector Kudu scooped up Lady Van der Kloot and gallantly carried her away while everyone else retreated as fast as they could, screaming and yelling. Mrs Bongo, shocked awake by the sudden deluge of cold water, struggled to manoeuvre herself under the cover of the breakfast table. She lay there on her back, totally bewildered and spitting out mouthfuls of water. Above her a large chunk of the ceiling collapsed and the waterfall became a hail of soggy plasterboard, insulation and broken tiles. Seconds later an unconscious man with no trousers on dropped through the hole and thumped onto the table. More screams rang out. No one was sure whether the man was dead or alive but he wasn't moving and looked a complete mess. Seconds later he was followed by a large, angry rhinoceros. Everyone stared in utter disbelief then panicked and ran in different directions.

"Gertie!" cried Fintan, glad to see that she hadn't been recaptured during the night, "Hello, old girl!"

The rhino had a strange look in her eyes. It was clear that the effects of the tranquilliser had now completely worn off and Fintan could tell she wanted her baby back. The table couldn't take any more. Its legs buckled and snapped, dropping the whole lot onto the flooded floor and ruining Mrs Bongo's hiding place. It also ruined Mrs Bongo! Gertie stamped her feet amid the shattered crockery and the remains of several breakfasts then charged wildly around the room. She swung her head at the abandoned dining chairs, scattering them like skittles. Then, as if things weren't chaotic enough already, a group of terrified cooks and waitresses came running in through the kitchen door pursued by ten very confused warthogs. Fintan had been wondering where they had gone. The kitchen staff ran straight into a crowd of fleeing diners who were running the other way to escape the mad rhino. More tables and chairs were upended and more crockery launched into the air. The warthogs, caught in the tangle of jostling legs, panicked and leapt onto the buffet table. There was an explosion of muesli, kippers and scrambled egg as they stampeded through the full range of breakfast foods on offer.

Inspector Kudu, his face splattered with a layer of South African porridge known as mieliepap, attempted to take control of the situation. He was immediately knocked to the floor by a surge of tubby executives trying to escape the chaos. His officers ran in hopeless circles, torn between arresting the diamond thieves, rescuing the guests and capturing the wildlife, without actually achieving anything.

At that moment another policeman arrived in the doorway to see what the noise was all about. He was holding a very agitated squealing, wriggling, baby rhino in his arms. Gertie's ears twitched at the familiar sound. How she could possibly have heard it amongst all the crashing, hollering and general mayhem is a mystery known only to mother rhinos. She whirled around, smashed a trolley loaded with jugs of fruit juice and galloped towards her calf. The policeman very quickly decided to let the little animal go, turned around and ran for his life. It seemed like the sensible thing to do.

The mother and child reunion was a wonderful sight to behold. The two animals nuzzled each other with surprising tenderness, grunting and squeaking with joy. Moments later they barged out of the door and trotted away to freedom. Fintan watched them go, feeling a mixture of joy and sadness then wiped a tear from his eye and a fried egg from his forehead. Gertie and her baby were going to be all right.

FIFTY EIGHT

The following day the Fedora family left the hotel and travelled to Johannesburg airport. It was time to go home. Every one of them looked thoroughly exhausted, glad it was over and impatient to be on the plane. They sat in the departure lounge amid a pile of suitcases, most of which were Felicity's. The poor girl had been making the most of her return to civilisation by treating herself to several new, expensive dresses to replace the ones that had been ruined by Mrs Bongo. Obviously new dresses needed new accessories to go with them so she had also bought matching bags and scarves and a dozen pairs of sparkly shoes. She still blamed Fintan for what happened to the old ones though and would never forgive him. She was also still seething about the 'dung incident'. Despite buying a range of the finest, most expensive hair care products in existence and washing her hair fifteen times, she was convinced she could still smell it. Mainly because

Fintan kept holding his nose and saying 'pee-yoo!' when she came near him.

Gribley was keeping himself busy by organising everyone's belongings, tickets and passports. He looked very pleased to be back to his normal duties which were much less life-threatening than escorting Fintan on his adventures. Flavian, meanwhile, was also beginning to return to normal. He had already said a few rude and obnoxious things about his younger brother which was an encouraging sign.

Next to him Mr and Mrs Fedora were both sitting in stunned silence. They were still having trouble believing that Fintan had paid back the enormous sum of money he owed them. It must have been some sort of miracle! The memory was still fresh in their minds of watching Suni sobbing into the hotel carpet as two very strong policemen wrestled the reward money from his trouser pocket. The thieving youth had since been taken away to a high-security hospital where his various injuries were being seen to under police guard. Mrs Bongo was there, too, of course. All the doctors and nurses had found her injuries very interesting as they had never seen anyone who had been squashed by a falling rhino before.

Fintan's parents were also struggling to believe that the previous day's chaos hadn't been the work of their youngest son. It was exactly the sort of mad carnage that he was well-known for causing. Wild animals falling through the ceiling of a luxury hotel and destroying the dining room had 'Fintan' written all over it. But according to the hotel manager, the boy hadn't been responsible at all! Apparently it was all the fault of the big game hunter, Mr Bok!

"So…" said Fintan happily, attempting to rouse his exhausted family with some sparkling conversation, "What about that old Mr Bok, eh? Fancy him getting so stupidly drunk he forgot to lock all his animal crates!"

"Indeed, sir," marvelled Gribley who suspected the wrong man had got the blame but didn't have any actual proof.

"I mean, what an idiot!" continued Fintan, "What on earth was he thinking, taking a live rhino up to his room? Must be a bit mad!"

Gribley made a vague 'hmm' noise without really agreeing.

Fintan seemed unnaturally happy. He could hardly believe how well everything had turned out; well, for him anyway.

"They say that when Mr Bok gets better the hotel management is going to make him pay for all the damage he caused. It's going to cost him millions!"

Mr Fedora sighed with relief. It was nice to see someone else paying the damage bill for a change. He looked up at the departures board and checked his watch. They were only half an hour away from boarding their plane and returning to their normal lives. Even Fintan couldn't mess *that* up, could he?

An announcement blared out over the airport's speakers.

"Attention all passengers waiting to board the flight to London, England," said a tinny voice, "We are very sorry to inform you that this flight has been delayed."

Everyone groaned. Mr Fedora folded his arms and frowned while Felicity kicked her little brother in the shins just in case it was his fault.

"Please accept our apologies," continued the announcer, "We will let you know the new departure time just as soon as we have removed the four zebras, ten warthogs and two rhinos which are wandering around on the runway."

THE END

Also written by Clive Goddard

Fintan Fedora the World's Worst Explorer
(search for the mythical Brazilian Chocoplum)
Fintan Fedora Explores Again
(Fintan Fedora & the Moon Dragon)

Also illustrated by Clive Goddard

Horribly Famous:
Pirates & their Caribbean Capers
Roald Dahl & his Chocolate Factory
Queen Victoria & her Enormous Empire
Inventors & their Bright Ideas
Leonardo da Vinci & his Super Brain
Darwin & other Seriously Super Scientists
William Shakespeare & his Dramatic Acts
Spartacus & his glorious gladiators
Winston Churchill & his Woeful wars
Boudica & her Barmy Army
Dickens & his Pen-Pals
Alexander the Great & his Claim to Fame
Julius Caesar & his Foul Friends
Sir Francis Drake & his Daring Deeds
Tutankhamun & his Tombful of Treasure

Just like Fintan Fedora, Clive Goddard loves to travel. And just like Fintan, his travels around the world have often ended up being a bit disastrous. He was once chased by an angry ostrich in Swaziland, stranded in the USA by a volcanic eruption and had his rucksack soaked by a leaky toilet in the Netherlands. He got food poisoning in Thailand, sunburn in Hawaii, heatstroke in Namibia and was bitten on the foot by a venomous spider in South Africa. He lost his camera in Tasmania, lost himself in Japan and got robbed in China (twice). He still loves travelling, though.

Before writing the Fintan books Clive Goddard was an illustrator for the Horribly Famous series and still draws cartoons for newspapers and magazines. When not writing or drawing or getting lost, Clive lives in East Oxford with his wife, two children, three cats and a giant slug named Bernard.

Lightning Source UK Ltd.
Milton Keynes UK
UKHW01f0844120818
327111UK00001B/12/P

9 780995 628724